03/21

TROUBLE WITH A TINY t

by Merriam Sarcia Saunders

CAPSTONE EDITIONS
a capstone imprint

Trouble with a Tiny t is published by Capstone Editions,
an imprint of Capstone.
1710 Roe Crest Drive
North Mankato, Minnesota 56003
www.capstonepub.com

Library of Congress Cataloging-in-Publication Data is available on the Library
of Congress website.

ISBN: 978-1-68446-281-0 (hardcover)
ISBN: 978-1-68446-351-0 (eBook PDF)

Summary: Westin Hopper gets in trouble—a lot. At home, at school, at his
grandparents' house . . . his ADHD brain always seems to make him to do
impulsive things. So when Westin finds a magic bag that makes his thoughts
come alive, he thinks it's the ticket to fixing his life. Instead, his wandering
brain strikes again, conjuring up a mini T. rex, an army of headless plastic
men, and a six-inch Thor. Now they all live in his bedroom, eating lunchmeat,
wreaking havoc, and growing, and Westin doesn't know how to make them
go away. But he'd better figure it out quickly. Tiny T is growing—and fast.

Image Credits: author photo by Tabitha Saunders; Bobbie the Chicken by
Sabrina Saunders

Designed by Hilary Wacholz

Cover illustration by Frances Castle

Printed and bound in China. PO3741

For my mother, Janet,
who always knew I would write a book.
- MSS

SUNDAY

One false move, and I'm dead.

Well, not *dead* dead. But if Pops hears me down in the basement, he'll blow like a volcano—angry, spewing lava everywhere. But, given what's down here, it's worth the risk.

I place my foot on the stair, careful to avoid the spot in the middle where it squeaks. I spend enough time visiting Gram and Pops to know the trouble spots. Silence. I take the next stair. And the next.

Crrkkk.

I freeze, listening for sounds from the living room above. There's nothing but Gram fiddling in the kitchen, Pops snoring like a lawnmower, and the dull hum of the football game Dad's watching.

I take another step in the dark. A single light hangs from the center of the room, and I hold my breath until I find the string. The bulb clicks on, dull and yellow, casting eerie shadows across the endless pile of boxes—stuff that belonged to Uncle Marty . . . before he disappeared three months ago.

I twist my ear up again for sounds that Pops might be heading to the top of the stairs to holler, "Dagnabbit, Westin Hopper! Stay out of Marty's things!"

But so far, so good.

Uncle Marty was an explorer and adventurer, always traveling to distant lands, slinking through hidden pyramid passageways, looking for buried treasure. All that treasure is here now, stashed in boxes. There could be a pharaoh's chalice. Or rubies and sapphires. Or maybe that mummified alien hand he told me he found during a dig in Albania. *For real.*

I seriously want to find that. The guys—Josh, Alex, and Frankie—would go crazy if I found an alien hand. Maybe Snake would stop being so mad at me for the basketball incident. I asked them to hang out today and help me look, but they had stuff to do. Snake didn't believe me about the hand, so now I have to find it for sure.

I step toward the boxes stacked in one corner, across from shelves filled with Gram's Christmas decorations and Pops's old records. It smells weird down here, like stale barf and old cardboard. Josh and I used to play in the basement when we were little, before Pops got all cranky. We'd always pretend it was a cave because even with the light on, it's still super dark.

I tap my thighs, spying around. Where would I stash an alien hand? Somewhere no one would suspect.

Next to the boxes is a giant taiko drum, which would be so awesome to bang on but would totally give away that I'm down here, so I don't. On a table next to the drum is an old green army box that says *grenades* across the side. Even *I* know better than to touch that. On top of that is another small, wooden box with a combination lock— the perfect size for a mummified hand.

I try to lift the lid—yay, not locked!—but inside is just a little key and some rolled-up papers. I glance down at the key, thinking. If I had an alien hand, I would definitely lock it up. I just need to find the lock this key belongs to.

I lift the key out of the box, and my other hand accidentally bumps the numbers on the combination lock. The lid slams shut. Good thing I don't need to get in there again.

I look around for things with keyholes. Over there! On the floor by some paintings is a small, blue, hard-sided case. Even in the dim light, I can see it has a lock. Score!

I slide over to it and kneel down on the cold cement floor, pulling the case toward me. I click the metal tabs. Locked.

I poke the key into the hole and—*aha!*—it is totally my lucky day, because the key fits.

I quickly click open the tabs and lift the lid. Turns out it's totally not my lucky day because the case is filled with boring clothes. No hand. No amazing, awesome thing that's going to change my life. *Darn it.*

On top of the clothes is a red velvet drawstring pouch with gold stitching. The pouch must be seriously old because one, it smells like stinky socks. And two, it's patchy and worn in spots—like something Gram might have put makeup in a hundred years ago.

I pick up the pouch to inspect. There's something stiff in it—a card, all yellow and worn around the edges. The print is faded but I can make out the words:

MADAME ZAQAR'S SHOPPE
OF
OCCULT CURIOSITIES
AND
ENCHANTED ARTICLES
GRIMOIRES. TALISMANS. AMULETS. WANDS.
CRYSTAL BALLS.

Okay! The first sign of something cool! On the back of the card, in creepy handwriting, it reads:

Beware: The purchased customized enchantment herein, conjured by the eye, is to be activated by one conjurer and passed down by blood. Purchaser hereby agrees to all terms of use (see indoctrination manual) and to do no harm.

Martin Q. Hopper

Purchased enchantment? Like, Uncle Marty bought something magical that apparently has a manual and terms of agreement and everything?

Now we're talking.

I dig through the rest of the case, pulling out all the clothes in search of something that looks like a grimoire, talisman, or amulet . . . except that I have no idea what the heck a grimoire, talisman, or amulet is. But all I find are shirts.

I sweep my gaze around the boxes of Uncle Marty's things, and my eyes fix on the creepy swamp painting that used to hang over the sofa in his fancy townhouse— the one with a bug-eyed crocodile staring hungrily at a purple turtle onshore. The painting, not the townhouse, obviously.

I have so many questions. What the heck is a grimoire? What does indoctrination mean? Where is Madam Zaqar's shop? Why would Uncle Marty hang such an ugly painting? Do crocodiles even eat turtles? Can *anything* eat a turtle? Probably not. Too hard.

I sneeze from a dust bunny and drop the pouch back into the now-empty case. I have to stop daydreaming about turtles and find this enchanted thing Uncle Marty bought before Pops wakes up and realizes I'm down here.

I start to put the clothes back in the case and—*yikes!* I jump back. Something is creeping around the open case in front of me. It looks like a massive spider. *What the—?* Not a spider!

No way. This isn't even remotely, conceivably possible. Not in the least, little tiny bit.

Waddling along the inside edge of the case is a *purple turtle*. Like the exact same one from the painting. A teensy version, the size of a gumdrop.

I lower my shaking hand toward it to see if it's real or if I'm crazy, but then I freeze—the red pouch is wiggling. There's a lump inside, and it's alive.

From the pouch's opening comes a snout, then two bug eyes, then claws! No way! It's a mini crocodile. *Like the one from the painting!*

The crocodile spies the turtle and—uh-oh, I think I'm about to find out if crocodiles *do* eat turtles.

"No, don't!"

Snap! Quicker than the flick of a rubber band, the crocodile clamps down and gobbles the poor turtle up like a snack. Then the crocodile looks up at me with his bug eyes, blinks, and slowly waddles back into the pouch like nothing happened.

My mouth hangs open wide enough to drive a truck through. *No, no, no way.* I did not just see that. The things in Uncle Marty's ugly painting . . . came out of this little pouch. They came alive and crawled . . . *Out. Of. A. Pouch.*

My heart thumps like a dribbling basketball as I stare down at the pouch—now completely flat—in the case.

I hold my breath, waiting to see if the croc comes out again. Or another turtle. Something. Anything. But there's no croc. No turtle. No nothing. Just the plain, red pouch—flat and empty—sitting there.

That did not just happen.

No way, no how.

But . . . what if it did?

What if this pouch is the enchanted thing from the card?

Holy gobbled turtle.

Who needs a boring alien hand to show the guys?

I found MAGIC.

STILL SUNDAY

I kind of want to stay down here and see if anything else crawls out of the pouch, but I'm pushing my luck as it is. Pops could wake up any second.

I shut the case with the pouch inside, leaving the clothes on the floor in a pile. If I can get more things to come out of this pouch, I'll need this suitcase to trap them. No one needs a tiny, chomping crocodile roaming around freely.

Arms clasped tightly around the case like it's a lifeboat, I slink up from the basement and into the kitchen. I peer down the hall toward the living room, checking to see if the coast is clear. Dad's still watching the game, and Pops is still making snore-y warthog noises. I need to find Gram.

"Westin, what have you got there?" Gram scares the pants off me from inside the pantry. She goes to open the oven door and pulls out a sheet of cookies. A blast of hot air hits me, which only makes me sweat more.

I grip the case tightly. "Just . . . this? It was downstairs."

Gram slides the cookies onto a rack with her spatula and looks at me from the corner of her eye. "Is that Marty's?"

I nod.

"What's inside?" She runs cold water over the empty cookie sheet.

I could lie. And I do think about it for a millisecond. But I can't lie to Gram. She's the nicest person in my whole world.

"It's empty," I tell her. "Except for a little red pouch that's also empty. But I'm pretty sure it's magic."

Then I wait, holding my breath.

"Magic, huh?" Gram asks.

I nod. "Can I keep it?" *Pleeeeeease*, I add silently.

Gram shrugs. "I'll tell you what. You sketch something for my fridge, and we'll trade. Marty's magic pouch for the drawing. And when he returns, you bring it back. Deal?"

My eyes widen. "Really? Gram, you're the best!" That's the greatest trade ever. I love sketching. It's the absolute only thing I'm good at. Except maybe baseball, which I'm not allowed to play anymore on account of a bat-throwing/nose-breaking incident.

I set the case by the door. "Don't let anyone touch this." Then I walk over to give her a hug.

"Ooh, I've got to get these hugs while I can." Gram pulls me in and squeezes me into her soft chest.

I squeeze her back. Gram is like a giant squooshy marshmallow. She even smells like sugar, probably from all those cookies. I don't mind hugging her, especially since Uncle Marty's gone, and she's sad a lot, even though I'm a little old for hugs.

Gram kisses my cheek and leads me into the living room, where Dad and Pops are. I'll draw something fast, I decide, then Dad and I can leave so I can get back to the magic pouch.

"Sit here. Draw while I finish folding." Gram eases onto the sofa next to a pile of sheets.

"Do you need help?" I sit cross-legged at the coffee table in front of my sketchpad and pencils, hoping she'll say no.

"No, sweetie, you just draw."

"Where have you been, buddy? You missed a great game." Dad's in a chair next to Pops, both of them up close to the TV. His phone pings, and he glances down at it.

"Nowhere," I answer. "Who's winning?" I start drawing, but mostly I'm thinking about the fact that a mini croc just munched on a turtle and then disappeared before my eyes.

"Thirty-four to seventeen, Patriots." Dad types into his phone.

Pops snorts out of his nap. "You were sitting there the whole time. Pay attention. Just like Marty, I swear."

Pops is always in a bad mood lately, especially where I'm concerned. He thinks I mess up a lot, make too much noise, squirm too much, break things. Which I basically do. I generally try to stay away from him.

"Oh, Pops, be nice." Gram winks at me. "It's not a bad thing to be like Marty, Westin. He was adventurous, artistic, and imaginative."

Uncle Marty *was* extremely cool. Whenever he'd return from one of his trips, it felt like Christmas and a trip to Disneyland rolled into one. He always had all these photos, stories, and awesomely cool things from countries I'd never heard of. He became a bush pilot and a spelunker—which is a fancy word for cave explorer—and he even summited Mt. Everest.

Then, about three months ago, Uncle Marty kissed Gram goodbye and said he was going on another trip. But he never called her and Pops, which he usually did every

Sunday night, no matter where he was. He just sort of disappeared. No one knows where he went.

After a while, Dad and Pops packed up Uncle Marty's stuff. I overheard Dad say he thinks Marty must be dead, but I know Gram hopes he'll pop back and surprise us. I hope so too because I super miss him. Uncle Marty always laughed at my zany noises and tousled my hair and said my mind is creative. He got me in a way no one else ever does. Definitely not my dad or Pops.

Anyway, now I totally see how he led such an amazing life. The dude had magic.

And now, so do I.

This pouch is going to change my life. I can't wait to show my friends. How the heck am I supposed to sit here and sketch as if the most incredible thing in the world did not just happen?

"Dad, can we go soon? Isn't it getting late?" I rush to finish the red-flamed fire monster I started earlier in my sketchpad, picking another pencil from the box on the table.

"Is that a monster made of fire?" Gram looks over my shoulder. "So real! Like he could leap off the paper and burn down a whole building." She chuckles. "Show that to your father."

I shrug. "It's okay, I guess." I hold out the drawing to show Dad. "Dad, can we go?"

His phone pings again, and he looks down to read the text.

"Philip." Gram scowls.

Dad looks up. "Huh? Oh, right. Looks good, bud." He glances back down at his phone.

Gram casts a knowing smile my way and offers me a pillowcase. "Here, sweetie. You can help me fold this if you're done drawing."

I take the pillowcase and set it in my lap. "Dad. Time to go?"

He ignores me and continues typing. I sigh and fiddle with the scissors from the pencil box, snapping them open and shut like the crocodile's jaws. I can't stop thinking about what happened downstairs. What made that croc come out of the pouch? What started the magic? The painting? Maybe if I—

"Westin Hopper!" Gram shouts.

I flinch. What I do? What?

I look down at the scissors in my hand. Then I look at the hole I made in Gram's pillowcase.

Dang it.

"Gosh dern it!" Pops grunts. "What'd you do that for?"

I slowly put the scissors back on the table. Why *did* I do that? "Sorry, Gram."

"Seriously?" Dad looks up from his phone and sighs.

"Can't keep doing stuff like that, West. You're eleven. Use your brain."

My brain. Ha! A normal kid's brain might have been like, "Dude, bad idea to mess with scissors and a pillowcase you're supposed to be folding while daydreaming about disappearing crocodiles." Then that kid would've said, "Brain, you are so right. Good thing you stop me from doing dopey stuff."

But *no*, not my brain. My brain is worthless. He's Vacation Brain. In Hawaii half the time. Or climbing Mount Kilimanjaro. Or canoeing the Amazon.

Wherever he is, he's not in my head doing his job.

"Gonna have to pay for some new sheets." Pops settles back into his brown lump of a chair. His wiry gray eyebrows close in on each other. "Teach you to appreciate the value of a dollar."

"I'm really sorry, Gram." I sigh, my face hot with embarrassment.

Dad stands and stretches. "Yeah, Ma, sorry. West will use allowance money for the sheets. Right, bud?"

"I guess." Hopefully the standing and stretching means we're getting out of here before I do any more damage.

"That was a good game, huh, Pops?" Dad pats him on the shoulder. "Gotta get going, now."

Finally!

Dad pulls his keys from his pants pocket. "Ma, thanks for lunch. See you next Sunday, okay?" He leans down to kiss her. "Bud, your mom'll be here soon. Can you stay out of trouble till then?" He leans over and messes my hair.

"Wait? What?"

"Don't forget your clothes and stuff. Tell your mom I'm going to email information on the private school I mentioned to her yesterday. We need to start the application soon if you're going to transfer. I'll see you next Sunday."

I bounce up and follow him to the kitchen. "Wait, Dad, I'm supposed to go to dinner with you. And what private school? Transfer?"

Dad's phone pings with another text, and suddenly I get what's happening—or rather, *who*. Cindy, Dad's girlfriend.

Dad grabs his coat off a kitchen chair. "We talked about the school, remember? This not paying attention is exactly why I want you to go there." He starts toward the door.

"Wait. I don't remember. And I thought we were going out for pizza, just you and me," I protest. If Dad leaves, I'm stuck here until who knows when. All the magic might be pouring out of that pouch in the meantime, spilling into nothingness forever.

"Next time. But tell Mom to check her email, okay? We need to get on that application." Dad doesn't look back as he heads to the door, moving smoothly, like an octopus gliding through water.

"But . . ." I say, except he's already gone. I watch through the kitchen window as he peels out of the driveway in the Evidence, which is what Mom calls his bright red sports car. She says that it's proof he could pay more child support.

I wish I were in that car right now.

I turn away from the window and eye the case containing the magic pouch. Maybe Mom will be here soon, and I can go home and mess around with it. My insides jump just thinking about it.

In the meantime, I grab another soda from Gram's fridge. Mom never lets me drink soda because she says it's like setting a Tasmanian devil on fire, whatever that means. So I always load up at Gram's. When I shut the fridge, one of my sketches—a hulky warrior fighting a dragon—falls from its magnet and floats to the floor. I gave that one to Dad last Sunday, but I guess he forgot it.

I pull my phone out and text Josh: **Dude, you will never believe what I found in Gram's basement**

I watch the screen for a few minutes, waiting for him to ask what, but he doesn't reply. Maybe his mom took his phone away. I go back into the living room to wait. Pops has fallen back asleep, and Gram is sporting a TV coma-glaze watching some goopy kissing movie.

This is so boring.

Come on, Mom. Where are you?

I look down at the hole I cut in Gram's pillowcase. *Sigh.* I'm such an idiot sometimes. I should probably get out of here before I wreck something else. "I'm going to wait outside."

Pops sits up suddenly and starts to push himself out of the sinkhole that is his armchair. "I'm gonna keep my eye on you out the window," he says. "Make sure you don't pop the blossoms off Mrs. Schauble's roses like that one time."

I flash a look to Gram, tapping my foot nervously. What if Pops sees the case and takes it away? I have to get the pouch home. I have to figure out how the magic works. I have to show it to the guys.

"Sit back down before you hurt yourself, Pops," Gram scolds him. "Go play outside, Westin."

I don't wait for Pops to argue. I scoop my sketchpad off the table, turn, and bolt out of the room. "Love you!" I yell over my shoulder.

"Don't forget your cookies," Gram calls after me. "And my drawing!"

In the kitchen, I pluck a drawing of a vampire-unicorn from my sketches and leave it on the table for Gram, then stuff the sketchpad into my backpack, which is spewing torn homework and old drawings from its opening. I sling it over my shoulder, practically holding my breath in case Pops manages to get himself out of that chair. I grab a grease-stained paper bag of cookies from the kitchen counter in one hand and the blue suitcase in another.

My duffle bag, filled with clothes and other things I carry between Mom's and Dad's houses each week, is on a kitchen chair. I knock it off with my foot and shove it down the back stairs. No sign of Pops, but depending on how bad his arthritis is, sometimes it can take him ten minutes to shuffle to the kitchen.

Slamming the door behind me, I race to the driveway, my feet barely touching down. I take a giant breath and glance at the back door and the kitchen window. All clear so far.

Come on, Mom.

I pull out a chewy, gooey cookie from the paper bag while I wait. Green and pink sprinkles go all over my shirt as I shovel the cookie into my mouth. *Mmm, these are good.*

After a bajillion light-years, I see a red Toyota slow in front of the house. *Yes!* Mom finally, finally pulls into the driveway and beeps her horn.

Time to get home and make some magic!

STILL SUNDAY—ABOUT
TO GET IN THE CAR

Mom gets out of the car and opens the back door to help me load my stuff. "Hey, squirt, Gram made you wait out in the cold?" She lifts an eyebrow. "What'd you do wrong?"

"Nothing. I swear." I gently place the case on the floor, and Mom hands me my duffle. "I just wanted to wait out here."

"What's that little suitcase?"

"Nothing. Cookie?" I hold the bag out to her, hoping to distract her.

She doesn't take one. "Did your father give it to you?"

"No. It's mostly empty," I say, which is the truth.

"Gonna organize my room a bit. Maybe put my baseball cards inside."

This is a good explanation for two reasons:

After I figure out the magic, maybe I *will* put my baseball cards in the case. Maybe I can even get mini baseball players to come alive from the pouch!

Anything about organizing my room will shock Mom into silence, and she won't ask me anything else about what's in the case.

Mom gets in the car.

Bingo.

"Is your father still in with Gram? Or did he go see *Cindy*?" she asks, clicking her seat belt.

I don't like to talk to Mom about Cindy. Whenever we do, Mom's voice gets high and tinny. Sometimes, she calls Cindy the *nanny*, which is a little weird. I guess because some days Cindy stays with me if Dad has to work. Cindy's okay. Mostly we just eat chips, watch TV, and don't talk.

"He had to go," I say as we drive off.

Mom makes a *hmmf* noise. "Did you get all your homework done before you and Dad came to Gram's today?"

I shrug.

"West? Did your father go through your planner with you?"

"I guess."

"You 'guess'? Hon, is that a yes or a no?"

"Sure. He did."

I know Mom thinks she's helping me, but most days she's like a question factory with the conveyer belt stuck on overdrive: *Do you have homework? Who did you eat lunch with? Did you turn in your math? Do you have plans after school? Did you bring your PE uniform home?*

Sometimes I imagine she's a human helicopter, hovering over me. The pilot's cockpit is her head as she whirs about me, spitting questions, making sure I remember stuff. *Whir, whir, whir.*

I stare out the window, thinking about my next steps. I don't know how this magic pouch works, but it made the turtle and crocodile come alive, so maybe it brings paintings to life? That feels like a good guess. I'm hoping it works on posters too. I have one of a white tiger with red eyes in my room, which would be awesome.

Oh, wait. That could be bad.

Maybe my poster of the Boston Red Sox, the most awesome-est baseball team ever. (My friends think that's weird because they all like the San Francisco Giants.) But a live, tiny baseball team? They'll think that's awesome no matter which team it is.

I wish Uncle Marty were around to tell me how the magic works.

"Do you think Uncle Marty's dead?" I ask.

Mom flinches and glances sideways at me. "Oh, West. Why would you ask that?"

"Dad thinks so," I say quietly. "He said Marty hasn't paid rent or used his credit cards or touched his bank account."

Mom's forehead crinkles. "He told you that?"

I shrug. "Overheard him."

She waits a beat, then says, "You miss him, huh?"

I nod, and Mom reaches over to run a hand down the back of my hair.

"Dad never wants to talk about him," I say.

Mom tilts her head. "Marty and your dad—well, they didn't always get along. But they both love you." She pauses again. "The truth is, I don't know what happened to Marty. I hope he's okay, though. Maybe he's off on one of his big adventures. That's what I like to imagine."

I like to imagine that too, but here's what I don't get: If Uncle Marty *is* off on one of his big adventures, why would he take off without his magic pouch? Maybe there's a reason he left it behind. Maybe it's a bad idea to mess with it. Maybe I should put it back. (After I make something come alive to show the guys, that is. Then I'll put it back.)

". . . a conference on Friday that I need to prepare for.

Will you be okay alone for a couple of hours after school if I'm late this week? West . . . ?" Mom takes a hand off the steering wheel and nudges my side. "Are you listening?"

I turn to Mom. I'm not sure how long she's been talking. "Oh. Sorry. Yes, sure."

I do feel bad for not listening. Except for when she's talking about Dad—or asking her seven thousandth question—Mom is pretty cool. She's forty, but people always say she looks way younger. What do I know, though? Most grown-ups look old. All I know is there are way more lines on her face since Dad left.

"You could use the time to start the essay for that charter school," Mom continues.

"Huh?" I whip my gaze up.

She sighs. "I'm sorry, West, but I can't keep paying the mortgage alone. It's just too much. We have to move to a more affordable neighborhood."

I hate when Mom says stuff like that. I know what she really means is that Dad doesn't give her enough money.

"And unfortunately, that means you'll have to change schools."

"Move? I don't want to move."

"There's a charter school, all about nature. You could transfer mid-year."

"Nature? Mom."

"It could be really good for you, West. Trust me. But you have to be accepted. I know they'll be very impressed by your artwork, but your grades need to be reasonable too. And you have to write an essay about why you want to attend."

Well, that solves that. I don't want to attend.

"Is this the same school Dad was talking about? I don't get why we can't just stay here."

Mom chews her top lip, which is what she does so she won't say something bad about Dad. "Uh, no. Your father doesn't . . . he thinks if we move, you should go to a different school—a very strict private one. Of course he's happy to pay for *that* but not to help with the mortgage."

I guess she wasn't chewing her lip hard enough. I don't know what to say. I'd way rather go to nature school than a strict school, but mostly I'd rather Mom and Dad didn't fight about it.

Truthfully, school isn't really my thing. Last year, after like a million self-management cards, Mom brought me to a doctor who said I have ADHD. That stands for attention deficit hyperactivity disorder. It's a really long name that basically means Brain is on vacation when I need him, so I do stuff that I can't control, forget to do my homework, space out when I should be focusing . . .

My best friend, Josh, usually thinks the screwy stuff I do is really funny—or at least he used to. But after basketball camp last year, he started hanging out with these new guys—Snake and Alex and Frankie. And lately things have been different.

I'm pretty sure it's because of the black-eye incident the first week of school. Everyone plays basketball at lunch, but one day I missed a pass. I guess Snake thought I was going to catch it, but I was sort of spacing out. The ball went right past me and hit Snake straight in the face. He ended up with a black eye.

At first, he said it was super painful, but then everyone else thought it was cool, so he did too. I don't know exactly why he's still mad—it's not like I did it on purpose—but it hasn't been the same since.

Just another thing ADHD has ruined for me.

Mom always says that having ADHD doesn't mean I'm not smart. *Yeah, right.* It's a month into fifth grade, and I've already failed a bunch of math tests and missed a bajillion history assignments. How am I supposed to know what's on the test? Or which page to do for homework? Or how to divide fractions? Vacation Brain is rafting the Nile while I'm at school, but no one believes me! Especially not my new teacher, Mr. Widelot.

Most days when I get home from school, I just stare at

my agenda, which is usually blank. I have no clue what I'm supposed to do. So I don't do it.

That doesn't seem very smart to me—or to Mr. Widelot.

"I probably won't get into your school or Dad's," I tell Mom. "My grades suck."

"Language, mister." Mom scrunches her face. "I think this new nature school could really improve your ADHD. I don't know how else to help you, sweetie. Maybe it's time to try some medicine? I've read a bunch about it online, and it seems to help a lot of kids."

I shrug. If medicine could shut down Vacation Brain's travel plans, it would be great. But Sherman Levine takes pills for his ADHD, and he says they make him feel like a zombie—without the people-eating part, of course.

Then there's the whole Dad thing. He says he doesn't want his son on *"drugs."* He thinks I just need to try harder, that I need more structure and discipline—which usually blows up into another fight between him and Mom. She thinks he's too hard on me.

I look out the car window at the trees whizzing by, thinking about what poster to make come alive in my room. Behind my bedroom door is an old Pokémon poster. That would be the most amaze-balls thing ever. I could put the magic pouch next to that poster and make a live Pikachu come out. I can trap it in the case, then invite Snake and Josh over to show them. Snake will think it's so rad, he'll *have* to forgive me.

I glance over my shoulder at the suitcase on the floor. Everything is about to change. Vacation Brain may get me into trouble with a capital T, but with Uncle Marty's magic, trouble is a thing of the past.

SUNDAY—BACK AT MOM'S

I run into my room straight from the car, slam my door, and set the suitcase behind it, right under the Poké- mon poster—the one with one hundred fifty characters. I leave the pouch in the suitcase, so when the Pokémon start to come out, I can trap them.

Barely breathing, I peer over the open lid of the case and look in. The red pouch stays flat and empty.

I wait.

Nothing.

I wait some more.

Still nothing.

Oh, come on.

I sweep books, baseball cards, and an old rubber

T. rex off a corner of my desk and put the case there, right under the poster of the Red Sox. I'd rather have Pikachu, but a baseball team is a solid second choice.

I open the case and take a step back. Closing my eyes, I say, "Ta da!" before opening them again.

Nothing.

Dang it.

I slam the case closed and a foot-high pile of Poké-mon cards spills over and lands on a bunch of clothes. Dumb magic pouch. Would've been nice if that indoctrination manual came with it or something.

"West! Can you please bring me your dirty laundry?" Mom calls.

"I'm sorta busy!" I holler back. I shove my hands deep into my pockets and stare at the pouch, willing it to do something, even if it's just the chompy crocodile again.

Nothing happens. Maybe posters don't work?

I run out to the living room.

"Westin, the washer is already started! Can you hurry, please?"

"Just a sec!" I grab a painting off the wall, the small one of a clown on a tricycle. I'm not a huge clown fan, and honestly, a tiny clown could be super creepy, but the only other paintings are of flowers.

"Westin, did you hear me?"

"Be right there!" I shove the little painting into the suitcase just next to the bag and cross my fingers.

"Don't make me come get it!" Mom's voice is up a whole octave.

Nothing is happening, so I blast out a breath, grab some dirty clothes, and kick my bedroom door shut behind me. Magic will have to wait.

After pizza and a movie, Mom goes through each item in my planner for the previous week—even though I told her I already did it with Dad—double-checking to see if I actually did everything. As soon as she releases me from her torture, I try putting the suitcase near the Pokémon poster again. I hold my breath and close my eyes, hoping maybe the magic just needed time to recharge.

Still nothing.

I even dare to put the suitcase under the tiger poster. The tiger would probably be tiny anyway, just like the croc—that could be mega-cool, like a man-eating kitten.

But the pouch just sits there. I try magazines with football players, the newspaper, and even the cover of a scary novel. Nothing comes out. Not even one, tiny half-eaten turtle.

Darn. I toss the case on the floor, shut off my light, and go to bed. Maybe the magic needs to charge overnight. Maybe tomorrow will be different. Maybe tomorrow I'll make something amazing.

MONDAY MORNING

"Shoes on, please!" Mom tucks a sandwich into my lunch bag. I don't move from my spot on the floor where Fiddles, the largest, laziest cat ever, is using her sandpaper tongue to lick maple syrup off my face. "Westin, please don't let the cat lick you like that. Go wash your face."

"But she loves syrup!" I give Fiddles a last chin scratch and gently nudge her off me.

"Hon, we were supposed to leave five minutes ago," Mom says. "You don't want another tardy, right? You've had seven, and it's only October."

Pretty much like every morning, Mom rushes around, getting ready for work, making my breakfast and lunch. I take about a thousand hours to get ready. Mostly because there are about a thousand things way more interesting that distract me: our cat, Fiddles, or bowling over my plastic army men with a tennis ball, or reading the sports page, or sketching. I did one of a giant two-headed spider with jagged fangs earlier this morning and tried putting it next to the pouch to see if it would come out. It didn't work either.

Anyway, that was probably a bad idea. Worse than the tiger, even.

"West, did you hear me? *Shoes! Now!*"

I shuffle down the slick hallway, working up enough speed in my socks to glide into my room like I'm on ice. *Whoosh.* I slide right into the middle of my room. That was awesome! I should try that again.

I slide back into the hall and glide back into my room, nearly slamming into the hamster cage on my floor. *Whoa!*

"*Westin!*"

Wait, why am I in here? I can't remember, but now that I'm here, I might as well try the magic one more time.

I kneel beside the case. There should be some sort of formula. . . . I just need to figure it out. I look at the old card from Madame Zaqar. Blah, blah, *conjured by the eye, is to be activated by one conjurer only and passed down by blood,* blah, blah. Not helpful.

Think. Think. I was in the basement, sitting next to the case, holding the pouch and thinking about—

Wait.

I was *holding* the pouch. Since I got home, I haven't actually touched it again. It's been in the suitcase so I could trap anything that came out. But in the basement, I was holding it and *thinking* about the crocodile and the turtle.

Whoa, whoa, whoa.

What if I have to be holding it for it to work? What if it's not the painting that made the animals come alive. . . . What if it was my *MIND?*

I lift the pouch out of the suitcase, squeezing it, hoping I'm right. I have to find out.

I leap up and head for the Pokémon poster, hopping over the rubber T. rex I threw off my desk last night. Ooh, a live T. rex could be—

"Westin Scott Hopper! What's taking you so long?"

Shoot. This'll have to wait. I gotta go to school! I drop the pouch on the floor and grab my black sneakers—the ones with the red stripes—from under a pile of clothes in my closet. I just about finish tying one shoe when something catches my eye.

There's a lump in the pouch!

I sit up straight. Then I inch over to it, moving on my hands and knees, my stomach clenched. The pouch isn't in the case anymore, so whatever this is, there's no way to trap it.

As I watch, the pouch wiggles, and a small, green scaly tail appears. The crocodile again? My shoulders slump. Maybe that's all it makes. Turtles and crocodiles. That's not nearly as awesome.

But then the lump stands up. Crocodiles don't stand.

The pouch falls open, and holy dinosaur! It's a ten-inch-high, *very live, very angry* T. rex. Just like the rubber one from my desk.

"I did it!"

"West, did you hear me? We're going to be late!"

The T. rex looks at me, then looks at my open bedroom door. He dashes for it, his thick tail swishing.

"Oh no, you don't!" I race to my door. I can cover a lot more ground with my long legs than a mini T. rex can. Even a super-fast one, like this guy. I slam my door shut.

"I'm counting to ten!" Mom hollers. "And don't forget your backpack. One. Two . . ."

My heart is throbbing in my throat, my back is against the door, and I'm facing a live T. rex. That I made with magic. And I'm late for school.

"Okay, you're really cool, but you have to go back into the pouch now."

The T. rex cocks its little head to the side, sort of like a dog who doesn't understand its owner.

"Pouch. Go in. Now."

But then the dino spies the hamster cage on my floor—more importantly, he spies Cappuccino, my hamster, running on the little wheel inside.

The T. rex's nostrils flare, and he bares his pointy dinosaur fangs in my direction. Then he makes a run for the cage.

I grab the whiffle bat leaning against my white bookshelf and start swinging. "Get away from her!" Right before the T. rex gets to the cage, I clobber him. He hisses, backing away.

"Ten! West, if I have to come get you, I swear, no TV for a month."

"Coming! Mom, I'm coming!" I put my left sneaker on top of the hamster cage and grab the handle, backing out of my room while I swoosh the whiffle bat with my other hand. Once I'm safely in the hallway, I drop the bat and shut the door.

Mom is right there waiting for me. "What are you doing with Cappuccino's cage? And a bat? Stop playing and let's go. Put your other shoe on in the car."

She shoves my lunch bag at me, then huffs out of the house, mumbling something about being late for work again.

I set the hamster cage on the coffee table and look back at my bedroom door. There's an inch-high opening between the floor and the bottom of the door. I cross my fingers that:

1. The T. rex is too large to fit underneath.
1. The T. rex is too small to wreck my bedroom.

There's nothing else I can do now. I race out the front door and flop into the passenger seat of Mom's car, breathing hard. As we pull away, I stare at our small, gray house—our regular, normal-looking house that now has, oh, just your average, ordinary, tiny T. rex running around inside.

"Put your other shoe on," Mom says.

I keep staring at the house. That T. rex is going to rip it to shreds.

"Where's your backpack?" Mom asks. "West?"

I snap out of my trance and look at her.

"*Again?*" She takes a deep breath, but her knuckles are white on the steering wheel. "I'm sorry, we don't have time to go back today. You'll have to make do without it. You know, West . . ."

Mom rattles on about tightening our morning

routine or whatever. But I'm not listening. I'm too busy wondering how the heck I'm supposed to pay attention at school knowing there's a live T. rex destroying my bedroom.

MONDAY—AT SCHOOL

The reason most of the fifth grade loves Mr. Widelot is because of Candy Fridays. On Candy Friday, if the class behaves all week and earns enough points, he chucks candy at us. Mini chocolates, hard candy, small bags of jellybeans.

I say *most* of fifth grade loves him—not *all*—because then I'd have to include myself. I dread Candy Fridays.

If my class doesn't earn the points, it's usually because of me. Mr. Widelot doesn't seem to get that Vacation Brain makes me draw in the margins instead of finishing my work or get out of my chair to get a piece of paper without asking or yell out an answer without being called on. I swear I don't mean to. But all those things deduct points.

We need twenty-five for candy, and if we're short, then Nicole King whines, "It's Hyper Hopper's fault."

On the Fridays we *do* get enough points, Mr. Widelot never throws candy in my direction. The rule is you must be seated, and whatever candy lands near enough to grab is yours. The kids sitting around me know they'll likely get nothing. The one and only time Mr. Widelot threw in my direction, he actually pelted me in the eye with a sour-apple candy.

This week's point tally is sure to be no different. Mr. Widelot stands in front of the class, like always, wearing a T-shirt with a math saying that—I don't know—is supposed to make us think he's cool or something. Today's is:

DEAR ALGEBRA,
STOP ASKING US TO FIND YOUR X.
SHE'S NOT COMING BACK.
AND STOP ASKING Y.

Mr. Widelot is definitely not cool. None of my teachers are. But they're not all awful. Mr. Lowde, my art teacher, is super nice—even though it's kind of funny that he whispers everything, given his name.

Mr. Widelot, on the other hand, is like his name—wide. As wide as Fenway Park. Probably from all that candy.

"Settle down, class." Mr. Widelot taps his whiteboard

marker in his left hand. "The field trip to the museum is Thursday, and I'm still missing a couple of permission slips from . . ." He leans over his desk to check. "Oh, only one missing. Westin Hopper."

Figures. I have the permission slip. In my backpack. In my room. Unsigned.

"Do you have it?" Mr. Widelot asks.

I shake my head.

"I need it by Wednesday, or you stay behind."

I know the truth—he's secretly hoping I forget to bring it in. Without another word, Mr. Widelot turns his back and starts writing equations and stuff on the board, spewing monotonous math facts in a tone so boring it makes my head hurt. I'm doodling jagged teeth, tapping my foot on the leg of Nicole's chair. *Thwap. Thwap. Thwap.* Thinking. About the small dino problem that I accidentally on purpose created.

Nicole turns around. "Cut. It. Out," she whispers.

"Mr. Hopper?" Mr. Widelot clears his throat. "Earth to Mr. Hopper?"

If I had a dollar for every time that he uses that hilarious Earth saying, I could buy a new brain.

"I asked if you have the answer to number four."

I put the pencil in my mouth and gnaw on the eraser end. Of course I don't have the answer to number four.

Even though I did the homework—for once—it's in my backpack, along with the unsigned permission slip. In my room. Getting eaten by a T. rex.

"Uh . . ."

Mr. Widelot stands with his whiteboard marker in the ready position, probably calculating how much candy he'll save this week because of me.

Nicole shoots her hand into the air. "I have the answer, Mr. Widelot." Her blond hair is so long it can get trapped between the back of her chair and the front of my desk. Sometimes I focus on her hair when I'm supposed to be paying attention to something else, watching as she inches her chair back, unaware any minute her hair will be trapped, and she'll scream, *"Ouch!"*

It's one of the highlights of my day.

The beige wall phone in the classroom rings, which means the office is calling, saving me from having to tell Mr. Widelot that I don't have the homework. He answers the phone and looks straight at me.

Uh-oh.

I knew it. The T. rex magically grew and now Principal Peckinpaw is calling to say that a T. rex is on the loose, and we all have to run for it. Vacation Brain strikes again. Seriously, a dinosaur? I couldn't just make Pikachu? Unreal.

"Mr. Hopper, to the office." Mr. Widelot hangs up the phone. His expression is a mix between annoyance that his class has been interrupted because of me—again—and relief that I'll be leaving.

The class breaks into "*Oooooohh*." They think I'm in trouble with a capital T. I probably am.

"Dang it." I slip out of my desk. Nicole has a total *nah-nah-nah-nah-na* look on her face, so I stick my tongue out at her.

"Mr. Widelot!" she cries out.

"Detention after school, Westin."

For that? He can't be serious. I can't have detention. I have a T. rex in my room.

Double dang it. Great going, Vacation Brain.

When I get to the office, I nearly crash into Mr. Lowde as he walks out.

"Oh, sorry, Mr. L."

"Westin, glad I bumped into you," he says quietly.

"You are?"

"I'm starting an after-school art club for my accelerated students. I'd like to invite you to participate."

I'm pretty sure I didn't hear him right, which—because he's so quiet—is very possible. Teachers never invite me to participate in special stuff. "Me?"

"Yes, of course you." He puts a hand on my shoulder.

"I'll be sending a permission slip by email to your parents. It's a commitment, three days a week after school. Think about it."

"Sure. Okay." I smile. This is unexpected and a really great reason to get called to the office.

I turn to go back to class when Mrs. Sandbeam, the office assistant, stops me. "Westin, where are you going? It's that time of year. A new Friendship Group." She points to the counseling room.

My lower lip curls. Ugh, that's why I was called here? I've done Friendship Group for the past three years. The teachers wait a month to see who's not adjusting, then they stick us all together. It's usually filled with kids who wear their pants up around their chests and only talk about banana slugs or super angry kids with attitude problems or ones who can't sit still long enough to stay out of trouble—like me.

When I walk into the counseling room, there are four other kids already there, gathered around a long, white table. The walls have posters that say:

"You can make a difference!" and *"Listen has the same letters as Silent."*

I take a seat next to a girl with long, red hair. She's new this year—in fifth grade like me—but I haven't met her yet. Across the table is Cranky Steve. He's in sixth grade, but he looks like he's in college. And he hates me. We were in Friendship Group together last year too.

Steve flares his right nostril as I sit down. "Great, Hyper Hopper for another year."

I'm not exactly happy to see him either. He's in a constant bad mood.

I tap my fingers on the table like I'm the drummer for my favorite band, Cheap Plastic Part. I have to drum. I can't stop myself. There's a buzz in my body, pinging in a million directions, coming out my fingertips.

Cranky Steve reaches over the table and grabs my hands. "Knock. It. Off. I swear. Another year of your table drumming, and I might have to kill you."

I slowly pull my hands away.

The girl next to me scowls at Steve and smiles at me. "I think you have good rhythm."

I look at her and squint. "Thanks?" Most people who can hear pretty much hate my drumming.

"I can do the spoons pretty good," she says.

"Spoons?"

"You know, you put them back to back, then bang on your knee. Spoons," she says. "We could form a band."

Cranky Steve looks at her. "Why are you here? I've seen you around. Thought you were normal."

The girl doesn't answer right away. She chews her lip

and looks at the posters around the room. Finally she says, "Anger issues. I punched a girl, and apparently, that's not allowed at this school."

Steve raises his eyebrows like this girl might be his new favorite person, but I can't figure out if she's serious. Before I can ask, Ms. Molly walks in. She was the Friendship Group leader last year too. She has a really nice smile, but she looks barely older than Cranky Steve.

"Welcome to this year's Friendship Group!" she greets us, sitting down at the head of the table. "We're going to be meeting on Fridays during first recess, but I want to introduce everyone today. Let's go around the room. Tell us your name, age, and grade, then tell us one true thing and one false thing about yourself. We'll guess which is which."

Ms. Molly claps her hands and rubs them together, like this might be the highlight of her day. She needs to get out more.

Evan goes first. He's in sixth grade, loves Bigfoot, and stares at the table the whole time. His lie is that he saw Bigfoot in Yosemite last year. He glances up, and I can see his one wandering eye. Kids call him Stink Eye behind his back. Maybe to his face too, which isn't nice.

Next is Cranky Steve. He cracks his neck and says, "I'd rather be in science class than here, this group is a waste of time, and I already have enough friends. You figure out the lie."

Ms. Molly laughs nervously and quickly moves on to Marjorie without letting us reply.

Marjorie has short, dark hair that's shaved up the back of her neck, and she mumbles. I have no idea what she says. She looks super afraid to be here, probably mostly because of the girl she's sitting next to—the one with the red hair and apparent anger issues.

I kind of don't blame Marjorie. The new girl sits with her hands clasped on the table, elbows splayed out, like she owns the room. She's even chewing gum and not trying to hide it. She has a baseball cap on backward, and when she turns her head, I see that it's a Red Sox cap.

Interesting.

When it's her turn, she says, "I'm Lenora Pickering. I'm ten, in fifth grade. My dad and I just moved to Grannie's, off Green Gulch Road, so we could help her with the farm. My mom was a famous ballet dancer, but she died when I was little." She taps her finger against her lips. "Um . . . oh, I raise chickens, and I'm entering a brown one named Bobbie in the county fair."

"I think the lie is that your mom died," Evan suddenly blurts out.

"Evan!" Ms. Molly looks as horrified as I feel. Marjorie

tenses, like she expects Lenora to punch Evan any second. I halfway wonder myself.

"I'm so sorry, Lenora. Group, do we think what Evan said to Lenora was an *expected* or *unexpected* behavior?"

"Expected or unexpected" are Ms. Molly's favorite code words. It's her way of teaching us to recognize when we do unusual stuff—stuff people think is more appropriate for a circus act or a cartoon character.

We all drone "un-ex-pected" and move on. I'm up next.

"My name's Westin Hopper," I start, bouncing my leg, which helps calm me a little. "People call me Hyper Hopper, but I don't like it." I look at Cranky Steve. "I'm eleven, and I'm in fifth grade because my birthday's in August."

"I'm eleven, but *I'm* in sixth grade," Cranky Steve says. "Did you get held back?"

"We don't interrupt, Steve. Let West finish." Ms. Molly says firmly but still with a smile.

"At least stop shaking the table." Steve makes a sour face.

I stop bouncing and pick up a rubber band that someone left on the table. My pinging buzz now comes out in elastic stretching.

"I love the Red Sox. And . . ." I'm supposed to come

up with a lie, but it's too irresistible. ". . . I have a live T. rex in my room."

Everyone laughs, even Ms. Molly. "That's the lie!" Evan yells, way loud.

By mistake, I stretch the elastic too hard, and it zings right into poor Evan's wandering eye.

"Ow!" His hand flies up.

"Shoot, I'm so sorry!" I shout.

"Great. Flick the kid with the bad eye." Cranky Steve leans back in his chair and crosses his arms.

Ms. Molly gets up and checks Evan's eye, which seems okay because it still wanders off in the wrong direction. She picks the elastic off the ground and tucks it into her pocket.

"All good. Evan's okay. West apologized. We'll just stay away from those elastic bands." She smooths her skirt and sits down. "Now, before our next meeting on Friday everyone has two tasks. The first—write a list of three things you're good at and why, plus one thing that's challenging and why, and turn it in to me. Then, before Friday, I want each of you to schedule a get-together with someone from this group for some time after school. I'll give you a few minutes to sort it out."

I cringe. I can't have one of these bananas at my house. Obviously.

T. rex. In room.

If I'm going to have anyone over to see him, it's gonna be the guys.

Marjorie turns to Lenora and says something softly, but Lenora's back is turned, and she doesn't seem to hear. Which is totally possible, given the whole mumbling thing.

Instead, Lenora tugs on my sleeve. "So, you like the Red Sox, huh?" She points to her hat, and I smile back. "Should we do this pointless get-together thing or what? You could come to the farm. Check out Bobbie the chicken. You know, meet her before she wins the fair and the fame goes to her head."

"Um." I tap on the table, and Cranky Steve glares at me.

"We have horses and stuff too." She shrugs.

"Sure. But not today. There's . . . something I gotta take care of."

"Tomorrow?"

I grunt, and she smiles.

And that's how I possibly make a new friend when I'm not looking.

MONDAY—AT RECESS

I complete the first Friendship Group task during recess.

What I'm good at:

> Art, I guess. Because I like it, it's
> fun, and Mr. Lowde says I'm good at it.

In class, when we have to write nice things about each other for Star of the Week, everyone writes, *You're good at art.* One time Lacey Franklin wrote, *You smell nice*, but I seriously think she thought Josh was Star of the Week, because she couldn't look at me for months.

> Baseball. I hit five home runs the
> last season I played, and my
> batting average was .350.

I haven't played in over a year, though. The coach said I had to take a break after I struck out and threw my bat so hard it hit Joseph in the face and broke his nose. I felt bad about that.

The third thing kind of stumps me. Not good at school. (Ha!) We probably can't use video games as one of our things. I don't skateboard (terrible at balancing), don't play an instrument (can't sit still through piano lessons), can't play chess (totally do not get that game), and have never been skiing (that's a disaster waiting to happen). So, I come up with this:

> Friendship. Even though I do dumb stuff like spacing out and missing a pass that gives my friend a black eye and makes him kind of hate me. That doesn't make me a bad friend.

At least I don't think it does. I'm not sure why I'm in Friendship Group all the time, but anyway that's okay. So, yeah, I'm good at friendship.

What I'm bad at:

Everything else.

MONDAY—AT LUNCH

"Quit shaking the table," Snake says.

We're sitting outside near the quad, eating lunch like most days. Our school is built around a grassy yard, and the classrooms open to the outside. Sometimes the guys eat at tables around the quad, sometimes on the field behind the quad, and sometimes on a grassy area by the basketball courts, which we nicknamed the Back Five.

Lately, because Snake's mad at me, the guys—Josh, Snake, Alex, and Frankie—don't tell me where they're eating. It's always a race to get my lunch and then figure out where they went.

Alex and Frankie look under the table to confirm

that I'm the table shaker. Of course it's me, bouncing like a superball, but I stop just in time.

Alex and Frankie are twins, but they don't look alike and play-fight all the time. They're Snake's minions. They laugh at all his jokes, dress like him—down to the same brand of sport socks—and do whatever he says. So, I guess if Snake is mad at me, they are too. Which is pretty dopey if you ask me.

Snake is really popular this year. My feet still don't reach the floor when I sit, but Snake has always been super tall, and he got even taller over the summer. Like he's an anaconda now, instead of just a plain old snake. Even the fifth-grade PE uniform is getting too small on him. He has acne and armpit hair now too. And lots of girls have crushes on him. Gross.

I take a giant bite of my PB&J and think while I chew. I'm waiting until Josh gets to the table to tell everyone about the T. rex. I can't stop thinking about it. After Friendship Group, I stopped in the office and asked Mrs. Sandbeam if there was any, like, out-of-the-ordinary news. Or anything. She told me to get to class.

But what if he escapes? What if he escapes and then grows super fast? I might have left my window open. If he climbs up my bookshelf, maybe his little T. rex arms could pry open the window, and he could squeeze out. It's only a few feet down to the ground. What if he escapes, grows super fast, and eats everyone?

My leg starts jumping again.

"Whoever's shaking the table, knock it off." Snake stares at me. "Where's Josh?"

"At the office. He's coming," Frankie says.

Someone lets a large one rip, and Alex howls.

"Nast-O. That was totally you, Frankie." Alex aims his crust at his brother's big head.

Frankie has a head the size of a pumpkin, and his face looks like a freckle-meteor crashed and broke apart on impact. Alex has a tiny head. I always picture Alex as one of those floppy, shaggy dogs with big, round glasses. Tripping his pumpkin-headed brother, seeds flying all over the place, as he smashes to the ground.

Ducking right, Frankie laughs and bats the crust away. It hits my face instead. Which is not awesome. Alex is eating bologna with mustard, and I can feel the mustardy crust stick to my cheek, then slide slowly down, leaving a gooey trail before it falls off.

The other guys erupt in wails of laughter. I wipe the mustard off with the back of my hand, then clean it off on my shorts. I laugh along with them—what else can I do?—and shake my leg more.

Frankie sticks his tongue out at his brother. "Nice throw, Alex."

Alex shrugs. "I don't know how I missed. Your head's as huge as one of those monster trucks at Snake's party yesterday."

"That was the best party ever." Frankie tosses a potato chip, and Snake catches it in his mouth. I feel like I have five thousand potato chips lodged in mine. What party?

"He's right, Snake. That monster truck rally was killer." Alex blows his stringy hair off his face and shovels pudding in his mouth.

Was this yesterday? Was this why no one could hang out? They were all at some monster truck thing for Snake's birthday, chowing awesome chocolate cake, without me? I suddenly can't eat anymore.

"Yesterday's was waaaay better than last year's rally," Frankie says.

What is happening here? My mind is being blown all over the place.

"You guys went to a monster truck rally for Snake's birthday last year too?" I ask.

Why didn't I go? Last year Snake wasn't mad at me. At least I don't think he was. Was he?

Before the guys can answer, Josh comes up to the table.

"Move over and make room," Snake says as Josh bends his wiry legs over the bench to sit down.

Josh and I have been friends since our moms met in a mommy's group when we were babies. Our hair is the same brown color, and when we were little, people thought we were brothers. Which was cool. Josh is taller than me now, but skinny, like the pole of a basketball hoop.

"Dude, did you see when the Devastator did that slap wheelie? That was so amazing." Alex high-fives Josh.

Everyone's talking about the stupid trucks, like, "Yeah! Legendary! Rad! That was so baller." Josh won't even look at me. How come he didn't tell me about Snake's party?

"What's a 'slap wheelie'?" I ask. No one answers.

"How about when the Hulk did that jump!" Alex hops off the bench excitedly and almost knocks his glasses off his face with his own hand gestures.

"Geez, chillax." Snake leans away from him. "I almost spilled my drink."

Alex quickly sits back down.

"Nimrod." Frankie laughs.

"That truck is like ten thousand million pounds," Josh says.

"Is it green? Is that why they call it the Hulk?" I ask.

"Duh," Snake says.

"I can't believe it made that jump!" Josh pretends to launch his sandwich off his lunch bag, flying it through the air—*whoosh!*

"I know, right? I totally thought it would land in the water," Frankie says. "*Kersplunk!*"

"Moron," Alex says. "It had tons of room to land."

Frankie kicks at Alex under the table.

I sink my teeth into my PB&J, even though I mostly feel like I want to puke. "Happy birthday, Snake," I say with my mouth full.

The whole table goes quiet. Josh pretends to find something interesting on the ground to look at. Alex nudges Frankie, and they snicker under their breath.

I swallow past the pit in my tummy. *Why didn't you invite me?* I want to scream. But no words come out.

Snake shrugs. "Thanks." He wads his lunch trash up. "This table shaking is freaking insane. Let's get out of here. Hoops time!" He stands, followed like robots by Josh, Alex, and Frankie.

"Yeah, man. Don't know why we put up with table shaking anyway," Alex says as they walk off.

"I don't know why we put up with *your face*, Alex." Frankie laughs.

"Oh, good one!" Josh high-fives Frankie as Alex tries to hip-check him from behind.

I stay and finish my lunch. I don't want to shoot hoops with them. Or see monster trucks crush cars. Who needs a truck to crush a car anyway? I have a T. rex. Maybe the first car he crushes will be Snake's.

MONDAY—AFTER SCHOOL

I sit in carpool, my knee bouncing, in the back seat with Macy McGee and Nicole King. They play Rock Paper Scissors, and the one who loses has to sit next to me. Thankfully they never talk to me and mostly pretend I'm not even in the car—unless it's to whine at me for wriggling or tapping my knees. *"Quit it. So annoying."*

The whole day was torture and mostly felt like there was a pack of lemurs in my belly, slipping and rolling around. I didn't stay for my detention, so tomorrow Mr. Widelot will probably find some way to humiliate me. Maybe make me stand in front of the class wearing one of his dumb shirts.

Before we get to my street, Josh replies to my message

from yesterday. Guess he was too busy with Snake's party to text.

J: **What did you find at Gram's?**

I'm still kind of mad at him for not telling me about Snake's party. If he doesn't tell me stuff, maybe I shouldn't tell him stuff.

Me: **Never mind**

J: **Are you mad? About the party?**

Me: **Coulda told me**

J: **Sorry**

Me: **Its ok**

I want to ask him why Snake didn't invite me, but I can't worry about that right now. I exhale a huge breath as we pull up to my house. It's still standing, so I guess the T. rex hasn't grown enormous, poked a hole straight through the roof, and escaped to terrorize the town—yet.

I ease open the kitchen door, hoping Cappuccino and Fiddles the cat haven't been chomped to furry bits of dino food. As soon as I'm inside, Fiddles comes from behind the butcher block and rubs against my calf. Whew! First good thing.

I peer into the living room and see my hamster cage sitting on the coffee table, right where I left it this morning. Cappuccino is still alive and well too—she's running on the wheel inside. Second good thing.

Down the hallway, my bedroom door is closed. Third good thing.

Mom will be home late today, so I have time to deal with whatever awaits me in my room. Before I dare open my bedroom door, though, I run to the coat closet and pull out the cooler, bike pump, baseball bats, and old cowboy boots before I find what I'm looking for—the butterfly net. It's probably not strong enough to hold a T. rex, but at this point, it's all I've got. Then I grab a handful of deli meat from the fridge. I hope T. rexes like salami.

I ease open my bedroom door, holding the net out near my legs in case the monster I created charges me. *Oh, crud.* My room is a disaster. Well, honestly my room is always a disaster, but this is even worse—totally trashed. My curtains are shredded at the bottom, and stuffing from an old bear is everywhere. Scattered across the floor are my green plastic army soldiers, their *heads* all bitten off.

"What the—"

The bottom desk drawer is marked with deep scratches, like the T. rex was trying to get in the drawers. Thankfully the window is shut. Whew! But I don't see him anywhere.

The magic pouch is in the center of the room where I dropped it this morning. Maybe the T. rex went back inside, like the crocodile did? I pick it up and look in, as if I can tell, which of course I can't.

Just then, a shape rushes at me from under the bed and grazes my right calf.

"Ow!" I drop the pouch and grab my leg. There's a bite on my calf—which stings—and I can see a little blood. "You bit me!"

The T. rex bares his pointy teeth, sort of hisses at me, and retreats under the bed.

I zoom to the bathroom and slather on the goop Mom puts on me when I get a cut. Who knows what kind of prehistoric germs are swimming in a T. rex's saliva. I slap a bandage on and head back in. On the bright side, at least he didn't grow super fast and eat the town or anything. Now I can tell the guys.

But . . . maybe I should send him back and start over. Make something way cooler. Less bitey. That's a better idea. That tyrant lizard's going into that pouch whether he likes it or not.

Holding the net out to protect myself, I push away the scattered army men on my floor and lay down a salami trail leading to the pouch, tucking one final piece of meat into the pouch itself. Then I stand on the bed, butterfly net poised to catch the T. rex, in case he won't go in.

Nothing happens. For, like, a long time. I kind of want

to lean over and look under the bed, but I'd also like to keep my face, so . . .

I grab my sketchpad and pencils from the backpack on the desk next to my bed. I might as well keep myself busy while I wait. I glance down at the poor half-eaten army men scattered around the floor. It would be awesome to have reinforcements—something to launch a massive strike and herd the T. rex back into the pouch. Kick his extinct butt. So, that's what I draw. A headless zombie army attacking a T. rex.

It's pretty good, gotta say.

Then, suddenly, the T. rex races out from under the bed and collects all the salami—man, he's fast. He doesn't even come close to going into the pouch.

I drop my pencil and dive at him with the net. He turns around, tilting right when I swish left, hisses again, and races back under the bed.

Well, that worked not awesomely. I climb off the bed and pick up the pouch. The last piece of salami is still inside. Dang it.

I kneel on top of the bed, holding the pouch, fiddling with the gold drawstring. If the T. rex won't go in on his own, I have to make him go in. If only I could use the army I drew.

Suddenly, the pouch gets heavy in my hand. Like

from out of nowhere, it has a bunch of rocks in it. Only the rocks are moving. Like a pouch full of wriggling spiders.

I toss the pouch on the floor before I have spiders or something crawling up my arm.

The pouch moves in waves, and then, one by one, live, green, headless army men come out. The zombie army! Righteous!

The men get into formation, as if they already know their mission, and march to attack the T. rex under my bed. The scraping and thrashing sound brutal.

I jump around, peering over the sides of my bed. One by one—*schwooff*—headless army men hurl out from underneath, bounce off the floor, and regroup to go back in for more reptilian torture. They're fierce, but they're no match for the T. rex.

I ease over the edge of my bed, peeking under to see what's happening. A huddle of army men surrounds the T. rex, trying their best to attack. He spots me spying upside down and lunges, his sharp teeth narrowly missing my forehead.

"Yikes!" I scramble back onto the bed.

From the hallway, Fiddles meows and scratches at my door to come in.

"Fiddles, get away!" If Fiddles was a hunting cat, maybe she would be feisty enough to catch the T. rex. But that's not my cat. I love her, but she's pretty lazy. Kind of fat too. The T. rex would probably gulp her in seconds.

I have to trap the tiny T. Maybe . . . oh wait, this is a great idea! Maybe if he won't go back, I could keep him—like Cappuccino, in a cage. Lots of people have lizards and stuff in cages. Snake would crash down my door to see that. I'd get invited to every birthday party in the world. Now we're talking.

Hard to explain to Mom though.

Anyway, I'll figure that out later. First things first.

I go to my bedroom door, watching as plastic army men continue to be shot into the center of my room before charging back under the bed for more. I carefully open the door, sticking my foot out to block Fiddles from coming in, and slip out. I'm going to need more deli meat.

I grab what I can—four slices of turkey, more salami, and all the disgusting bologna with the gross white blobs.

Fiddles is still pawing at the door when I return. I know why she wants in—she loves to curl up in the sun on my bookshelf, right under the window.

"Sorry, girl, not today." I block her. I feel bad, but this is for her own good.

I open the door and slip in, but before I can get it closed, Fiddles shimmies in, scuttling between my legs.

"Fiddles, no!" I drop the deli meat and grab her by the belly.

"*Riaow!*" She wriggles free and zooms over to the bookshelf, totally not caring that an army man torpedoes her in the face.

Hearing the commotion, the T. rex sticks out from the warzone under my bed.

"Look out!" I shout.

Fiddles casually looks right, face to face with the T. rex and his shroud of climbing army men. He's a teensy bit smaller than her, but who cares? He's a T. rex!

"Don't you touch my cat!" I cry.

Fiddles just *stands* there and licks her shoulder. Like she couldn't care less that there's a ferocious dinosaur snarling under the bed, less than a foot away.

I grab my whiffle bat to wham the T. rex if he attacks her. But he stays under the bed—like he doesn't know what to make of this giant furry thing—while the army men crawl over him.

"Come on, Fiddles. Come here," I coax.

Finally, some sort of survival mechanism kicks in. Fiddles flattens her ears and hisses. The T. rex flinches and scurries farther under the bed.

I swoop in and grab Fiddles, tossing her out and slamming the door. I look back, heart pounding. The tiny

T. rex is still in retreat. Geez, Fiddles has no idea how close she came to being prehistoric pet food.

Side-stepping the army men hurling at my shins, I pick up the deli meat and think. The T. rex obviously has no interest in going back where he came from, but maybe I can at least trap him someplace else—somewhere he won't eat my face off—until I can get rid of him.

I lay a trail to the inside of my closet, pushing the sliding door open wide. Then I jump up on my bed and wait, eyes stuck on the first slice of turkey.

In seconds, I hear the scrabbling of foot-claws. Not as fast as before because now Tiny T is pushing through a pile of army men. He forges through the swarm, shooing them off him like flies, gobbling up each slice of meat. He's slowing down. Maybe the attack is weakening him.

As he gets close to the closet, I drop down to the floor. If he looks back, I'm dead. Possibly for real.

Tiny T munches on the last slice before the closet. Then he stops.

Crud. *One more step, come on. Right into the closet you go.*

He kicks his thick hind legs to toss off an annoying army man and moves a step forward, into the closet.

As quick as I can, I race to slide the door shut. The T. rex looks up from his snack, his eyes wide, and turns to flee. I thrust my foot to block his escape, and he bites my sneaker, barely missing my toes. *Yikes!*

I slam the door on my foot, the T. rex's snout still stuck on my sneakers. I jiggle, trying to twist free, but his clench is fierce. Frantically I chuck my foot forward, flinging the T. rex off into the closet's back wall, and quickly slam the door. The T. rex—and all the army men—are shut inside.

I slump down on the floor and look at the dino teeth marks on my (used-to-be) brand-new sneakers. Then I glance over at the red pouch. I have the coolest magic that can create anything, and what did I make? A ten-inch-tall, violent, uncooperative T. rex and a useless band of headless, immortal army men.

What was I thinking?

Oh, that's right. I wasn't.

Vacation Brain strikes again.

MONDAY NIGHT

I have to come up with a story that will keep Mom out of my room. Not easy considering she likes to tuck me in at night and shows up from out of nowhere to put laundry away or vacuum.

I'm at the dining room table finishing my homework when her car pulls into the driveway. She always shops on Mondays, so I run out to help her with the grocery bags.

"Westin Scott, what a nice surprise. Thanks for helping without me asking." Mom hands me a heavy paper bag and the carton of milk. "Is your video game broken or something?"

"Did you buy deli meat? Like, lots of deli meat?" I follow her into the house.

"Sure, are you hungry? Help me unpack." Mom unloads the bags onto the kitchen counter, and I exhale when I see the deli packaging.

"How was school?" she asks.

"Fine." I always say that because if I don't, then the rotor blades on Mom's helicopter will fire up. She'll want to talk about it, and who wants to talk about school any more than you have to? "Oh, almost forgot. There's a homework thing I have to do at some girl's house tomorrow after school. For Friendship Group."

"Do I have to pick you up? Who is this girl? Can you write down her address and phone number, so I know where you are? Maybe I should call her parents first."

I can feel the wind as Mom hovers.

"Mom. I don't know. It's just some girl. I'll text you. And sign this. It's for a field trip on Thursday." Thankfully the T. rex didn't eat my backpack. I'm not getting stuck at school while everyone else goes on a field trip. "Oh, and Mr. Lowde wants me to do some art club. After school. Can I? He's emailing the permission slip to you and Dad."

Mom puts the cereal away and takes the pen from

me, scribbling her name. "An art club? That's nice. Get going on your homework. I'll start dinner."

Right about now is usually when I'd groan, drag my messy backpack to the dining room table, and find a million distractions before starting the work. If I even remembered to bring it home. I *never* finish my homework before dinner. By ten o'clock, homework that should have taken forty minutes has dragged on for hours.

But today is different. I had to finish my homework, so I could stay on high alert and keep Mom out of my bedroom. Amazing how motivating hiding a T. rex is.

"I already did it." Well, the parts I brought home. Pretty sure I left the science worksheet at school. . . . or lost it.

Mom stops unloading and looks at me like I have pizza growing out of my nose.

"Why are you looking at me like that?"

"You finished your homework? Do I need to check your planner?"

"No, Mom. Promise."

She decelerates slightly, thrown off guard. "You're just full of surprises."

Yes, I am. Full of surprises. My room is anyway.

"Now we'll have time after dinner to look at that

charter school application." Mom walks to the fridge, balancing a carton of eggs under a head of broccoli and three yogurts. I run to catch the yogurts about to fall off and open the fridge before she drops it all.

"So helpful tonight." She smiles.

A thumping sound comes from my room. Uh-oh. Someone's not happy to be trapped in my closet.

"You hear that?" Mom asks, ear cocked.

"Um . . ."

We're quiet, and the thumping stops. *Phew.*

"Huh. It's gone," she says.

"I can't do the application thing tonight," I say before Mom can ask any more questions.

"Why not? You said you already finished your homework. I'd like to get it started before your father—I mean, we just shouldn't wait, is all."

"I'm going to start cleaning my room. I swear. Remember that blue suitcase I found at Gram's house? It sort of inspired me."

That ought to distract her from the school wars with Dad.

"Really?" Mom crinkles her forehead like I'm speaking Chinese. "What are you up to?"

"Nothing. But . . . I don't want you to go in until it's done. Not under any circumstances, until I say so."

Mom puts a pan of water on the stove to boil. "What about hugging you good night?"

"All good night hugs will have to happen outside the perimeter." I stand with my hands at my hips.

"And if I have laundry to put away?"

"Leave it at the door. I'll put it away."

Mom puckers her lips. "Westin. Seriously?"

"Have a little faith." Ha! I can't even get in my closet.

Mom gives me a look. "Well, can you at least put Cappuccino back in your room? Her cage is making the living room smell funky."

"No!" I almost lost one pet today already. The T. rex would probably stick his tiny dinosaur arms through her cage and terrorize Cappuccino into a little hamster heart attack. "I mean, that's all part of my organizing and cleaning. She needs to stay on the coffee table. Just until . . . how about until I go to Dad's next Sunday? Please?" At least I *hope* this nightmare is over by then. "And don't let Fiddles in my room. I'm serious. No one is allowed to touch, look at, or breathe near my doorknob until I say so. Pinky-swear promise? I want to surprise you."

Mom stops stirring the macaroni in the boiling water and looks at me. "All right, I promise. But what has gotten into you? Homework is done, you help with groceries, and now you're cleaning your room. Has an alien taken over your body?"

No, a T. rex has taken over my room. At this point, the alien option might be better.

TUESDAY—AT SCHOOL

I'm wearing the same underwear as yesterday. Like I care. I have bigger problems. I'm super sleepy, since I got no Zs—not with T. rex and friends waging World War T most of the night.

As we file out of Mr. Widelot's class—where I shock-and-awed him by remembering my permission slip—Nicole turns around and says, "Ewww, you smell funny."

It's probably true. I probably do smell funny. My basketball shorts have some kind of giant red stain on the front, possibly spaghetti sauce from last night. Plus the mustard from yesterday. And even I can smell the B.O. on my Red Sox jersey, because I wear it all the time.

Like I said: bigger problems.

I hurry to my cubby to get my lunch, pull it out, and slam my cubby door. The guys are already sitting at one of the smaller tables in the quad, so someone needs to slide over to make room for me. They don't.

"Hey, guys." I stand behind Josh. "Can you move over, Josh?"

Josh doesn't move. What's up with him lately? I've decided I'll forgive him about the party thing and tell him about the T. rex, but not if he's going to act weird.

Snake looks up from his sandwich, makes a face, and exhales, which causes Alex and Frankie to sigh in unison.

"Told you we should sit somewhere else," Alex says.

"Josh?" I ask again, and he slides right a little.

I thump down onto the plastic bench; its surface is cold against my butt and legs. Even though it's October and kind of chilly, we all wear basketball shorts and T-shirts. Mom's always asking me to put long pants on, but I do not get what her problem is.

"Geez, now we're completely squished." Frankie elbows me and grimaces. "Maybe next time someone'll catch a clue about whether he's in or out."

"Maybe we wouldn't be squished if your head didn't take up so much room," I mumble.

"Oh, *snap!*" Alex laughs. "Good one."

"So, I'm going to blow up my house after school," Snake says. "You guys should teleport in and watch."

"Dude, seriously?" Frankie asks. "You've been building that, like, forever."

"I've loaded a bazillion wads of explosives, and it's ready to blow. Gonna be epic." Snake frowns my way. "Geez, man, quit shaking the table."

"Can I watch?" I ask.

"I'm going to blow the sheep up too. Everything."

"Beastly!" Josh reaches over the table to high-five Snake. "I'll turn on cheats, and teleport in."

"What time are you going to do it?" Alex pushes his glasses up his nose. "We're not allowed on the computer until after we finish homework."

"Whose server is it on?" I ask. I look at Josh, but he won't make eye contact.

"I'll text when I'm ready and wait until all you guys are there," Snake tells them.

"What's the IP address?" I ask. "Josh?"

Frankie leans his giant head over and whispers to me. "Hello? It's a private server."

"No duh. Hey, Josh, text me the address?" If anyone will tell me, it's him.

"Look up the definition of *private*, Hyper," Frankie whispers.

"'Look up the definition of private,'" I mimic. I can so top a video game explosion. "I have a live T. rex in my room."

Everyone goes quiet.

Snake rolls his eyes at Josh. Frankie swats Alex on the arm, and they snicker.

"No, really. I do."

"Sure you do," Snake says. "It's probably gnawing on that alien hand you said your uncle had."

"I swear. It crawled out of a magic pouch I found at Gram's. I made it come to life." I look from face to face. They're leaning away from me like I'm contagious. "Look, he bit me. And my sneakers."

I lift my knee to show off the mark on my leg and shoes, but I accidentally nudge Josh. He spills his drink everywhere.

"Dude!" Josh looks annoyed.

"Godzilla's in my room," Alex laughs. "He crawled out of my mom's purse."

"And I have the Loch Ness monster in my bathtub," Snake says. "Lean over the edge and maybe he'll eat your face off." He pretend-coughs "doofus" into his fist.

"At least then our annoying torture will finally be over," Alex says.

What's he talking about?

Josh shoves the last of his sandwich into his mouth

and scrunches his lunch bag into a wad. "Hoops time, animals." He does a three-pointer into the trash can and jumps up from the table. Everyone follows.

I'm not done with my lunch yet, but I throw it away too and run after them. "Wait up!" I can tell they don't believe me. Whatever. None of *them* has a T. rex in their room.

I catch up to Josh. "Hey, you should come over this week."

"This week? I don't know. . . ."

"You can see the T. rex. You gotta believe me."

Snake snorts a laugh.

"Sorry." Josh starts to walk faster. "Basketball practice."

"Every day?"

He runs onto the court. "Yeah," he says over his shoulder. "It's a special league."

"But it's really amazing."

"Take a picture and show me."

Snake throws Josh the ball, and he does a layup. There are ten boys on the court already, so I sit on the grass and watch.

A picture. *Why didn't I think of that?* I should've taken a photo with my phone before I trapped the T. rex in my closet. Then they'd *know* he was real.

Someone knocks my baseball cap off from behind.

"Hey." It's Lenora. "You're coming over today, right? The Friendship Group thing?"

I sigh. I'd rather get home to the T. rex, so I can take a picture of him for Josh. "I guess."

"Since we have to get it over with, meet over by the library after school. My dad will be in a blue pickup truck. See ya."

She walks back toward the quad, and I check if any of the guys saw her talking to me. None of them seem to notice or care. All eyes are on Josh as he takes a long shot. It swooshes through the net.

"Hey, can I play soon?" I yell.

No one answers.

TUESDAY—AFTER SCHOOL

Lenora's hand flies to her mouth like she might cry. Or puke. In the center of the mahogany dining table lies her prized chicken, Bobbie—cooked, on an orange-and-blue platter, surrounded by steaming broccoli.

"Grannie! NO!" Lenora walks to the table to get a closer look. Her voice is thin and shaky. "You *cooked* Bobbie?"

The minute we got out of her dad's truck, Lenora practically dragged me to the coop. Her face turned ashen when Bobbie wasn't there—like she knew.

"That bird was a menace. Meanest of the bunch," Grannie says. She slams the masher into the pot of potatoes, stirring and banging the edges. "Hand me the cream."

Lenora's face turns Red Sox red as she shoves the

cream at her grandmother. Her eyes fill, and I wait for her head to pop off at the neck.

"But—it was *Bobbie*." Lenora wipes her eyes with the back of her hand. "Couldn't you have picked Jojo? Or that ugly one we never bothered naming?"

"I don't name my food, child. That's you. Now put the glasses on the table and call your dad down for dinner. And use your loud voice. Man's got his mind in the clouds, I swear."

Lenora's head hangs as she slams the glasses on the table, and I wait for one to shatter. She rattled on about Bobbie the whole ride home from school. Turns out she *was* entering Bobbie into the county fair, like she said in Friendship Group. The lie was that Bobbie was a *brown* chicken. Bobbie was white—before she got cooked anyway. Now she actually *is* brown.

"Who's this?" Grannie wipes her hands on her apron and reaches out to shake mine. Hers is sticky and rough. She eyes me head to toe with the same sharp blue eyes as Lenora. Bet she and Pops would get along.

"West." Lenora's lower lip sticks out and quivers a little. She glances back at poor Bobbie. "How could you? I loved her." Her voice gets quiet.

"Me too. Mmm, mmm, good." Grannie lets out a cackle, and I jump.

Lenora darts daggers at Grannie and stomps toward the stairs. "DAD! DINNER!" She comes back and pulls on my sleeve, yanking me to the back door.

"Don't go all pouting and sulking," Grannie says. "Makes your face look like a raisin."

"You cooked my favorite chicken!" Steam puffs out of Lenora's ears. "Mom would have *never* done that to me. She loved animals!"

"Ha!" Grannie slops the pot of potatoes into a bowl, and it lands with a thud.

"What's that supposed to mean?" Lenora stops in her tracks.

Grannie tosses her pot into the sink. "Ask your father. Where *is* he, anyway?" She looks at me. "You staying for dinner, young man?"

Lenora growls in frustration. "No!" The screen door squeaks as she pushes it open, and it slams hard behind us.

"Isn't it early for dinner?" I ask. It's only four-thirty.

"They eat early. Farmers. Come on."

Lenora continues pulling on my sleeve until we get to the barn. Once there, she leans over the wooden corral and kicks hard at the bottom of the post. A waft of dust and rocks blows up and startles a brown horse slurping at the trough.

"I hate it here. And I hate her. She knew I loved that chicken." She scrunches her face hard, like she's trying to hold back tears with sheer force.

I don't know what to say. I'm not crazy about my own two-house family either, but I'm not going to talk to her about it. "Sorry," I say. I stand there, not sure what to do with myself. I wish I'd worn shorts with pockets. Stuffing my hands into pockets is always a great fallback.

"We live in this awful place because Dad thought the farm would be better than the city. Fresh air or something." Lenora continues kicking the dirt, and I choke at the chalky inhale of dust. "Stupid farm."

"Oh." Best I can come up with.

"I had friends at my old school. People aren't nice here. Girls especially. Bunch of Barbie dolls. They say I'm bossy. *Me!*"

"Really?" I fiddle with the fence latch because I don't know what else to do with my hands.

"Don't touch that!"

I yank my hands back. "What?"

"You'll unhinge it, and the horses will get out."

"I wasn't going to . . . sorry." Yeah, why would anyone call *her* bossy?

"You know we're in this group because they think we have social problems. They call it Friendship Group, but

Ms. Molly's just trying to teach us to behave like all the other robots. *'Group, is that expected or unexpected behavior?'"* Lenora adds a nervous smile, a great impression of Ms. Molly.

"Guess maybe punching that girl was a bit *unexpected*?" Crud, maybe I shouldn't have said that.

But Lenora laughs. "I just said that to get Steve to back off."

I laugh too. Guess I'm not the only one who doesn't like Friendship Group . . . or Steve.

"So, you didn't punch anyone?" I ask.

She glances sideways. "Well . . . maybe I shoved her a little. Mom did mixed martial arts, so that kind of reaction is a genetic instinct. Couldn't help myself. But anyway, she deserved it."

I raise an eyebrow. Her mom did ballet *and* martial arts?

"She said I should try dressing more like a girl."

"That's silly." The Red Sox cap goes without saying, and she also has on perfectly fine soccer shorts and sneakers. Totally legit. "Some people don't know what they're talking about."

That makes her smile. "I know, right? Grannie says I have to go to the group, so they can keep an eye on me. To make sure I'm *adjusting*." She uses air quotes around the last word. "What's your deal? You seem regular. Why do you have to go?"

"I dunno." I scratch my scalp. I hope this doesn't drag on too long. Lenora is nice and all, but I have a formerly extinct creature wreaking havoc on tiny plastic men in my closet. I need to get this over with and get back to my small dinosaur problem. "I don't pay attention well. And I can't sit still. I have ADHD. I do stuff and say stuff without thinking first and wind up getting detention. Which I was supposed to go to but didn't, so I'll probably be in worse trouble now. It's like my brain is on vacation. You're new, so maybe you didn't see Snake's black eye the first week of school? That was Vacation Brain's fault."

She nods. "Yeah, I saw it. What happened?"

"Alex threw a hard pass when we were playing basketball, and Snake thought I was going to catch it. But I was zoning out, and it went right past me. Into his face."

"Ouch."

"Snake's so mad at me, he didn't even invite me to his birthday party. He thinks I'm annoying now."

"Wow, I'm sorry. Why do they call him Snake, anyway?"

"He brought a pet snake to show-and-tell in kindergarten. It escaped, and the whole school went nuts.

No one ever found it, and he became 'that snake kid.'"
I shrug. "That was before we were friends."

"Hope the snake lived happily ever after," Lenora says. "Who else are you friends with?"

"Josh Farmer. Since we were babies. He became friends with Snake last year and so I did too. Snake has been friends with these guys, Alex and Frankie, since preschool. So we all sort of hang out."

"Sort of?"

"Well, I mean, I never do anything with just Alex and Frankie. Or with Snake without Josh," I say.

"If you never do anything alone with them, it doesn't sound like you're friends. It sounds like they're Josh's friends, and you tag along." She shrugs. "Just sayin'."

She doesn't know what she's talking about. "No, we're totally friends. They're just mad because of the basketball thing."

Lenora makes a weird face, like I said something that makes no sense. I get that a lot.

"I think you'd be an interesting friend, all fun and impulsive," she says. "Who knows what you'd do."

"I guess." I pause. I'm all for making a new friend, and it's cool looking at her farm animals, but . . . I gotta go. "How much longer do you think we have to do this? You think it's been long enough?"

Lenora flinches, almost like I punched her. "You're kidding, right? Is that what you mean by saying stuff without thinking? Because that was super rude, and I was just starting to like you." She turns back to the house and marches off. "Dad! We need to drive this joker home. Now!"

Dang it. Gosh darn Vacation Brain seriously needs to check out of the Ramada Inn and check back into my head.

TUESDAY–LATER

Lenora and I rattle down the gravel driveway in her dad's old, blue pickup truck, me sandwiched between them in the front seat. Lenora stopped talking to me the instant I asked when the hangout would end. Geez, it was just a question. She made her dad gobble his dinner down in two seconds so he could drive me home. Guess she's bossy at home too.

Mr. Pickering has close-cut hair and a scruffy mustache that looks like a fat caterpillar hanging over his lips. "Awfully nice of you to come over, Westin!" he shouts over the truck's loud engine.

Lenora looks out the window, leaning away so no part of her touches any part of me. That's fine with me but difficult because the ancient truck doesn't have the smoothest ride. I keep bouncing into her.

"You play sports?" Mr. Pickering asks, glancing briefly at me while trying to keep his squinty eyes on the road.

"Baseball. At least, I used to."

Lenora crosses her arms.

"Used to?" he asks. "That's too bad. Lenora used to play softball. Maybe you could 'used to' play ball together sometime. Happy to coach you. I 'used to' know a thing or two about it."

"Ah . . ."

Lenora turns even more toward the window. I don't think we'll "used to" be doing anything together.

"Nora doesn't know anyone yet, so I'm glad she's finally made a friend. It'd be real nice if you'd watch out for her at school," her dad continues. "She's a little grumpy sometimes, but she can be lots of fun. Can't you, Nora bear?"

"*Dad!*" Lenora juts her chin out, then turns back to the window.

"Okay, okay. Just trying to help."

We drive on in awkward silence.

"Um . . ." I glance at Mr. Pickering, then at Lenora. "You mad at me?" I say under my breath, as low as possible over the gravelly engine. I didn't mean to hurt her feelings and make her so upset. Who knew she was actually taking this Friendship Group seriously?

No reply.

"It's just . . ." I shift so I don't knock into her again. "I have a lot of homework."

"So do I."

"Which is why I figured you didn't want to do the hangout thingy for long either."

"Whatever. You don't get it."

"Sorry. I have . . . a lot going on. My parents got divorced. And my favorite uncle is missing."

"Yeah? Well, *my mom* is dead."

Crud. She's got me there.

Before I can stop myself, I start blabbering. "Well, also, uh, I found this thing at my gram's house, and it . . ." I glance at Mr. Pickering from the corner of my eye to make sure he's not listening. I should just quit talking, but of course, I don't. "I made something. I don't know how to get rid of it. It's kind of dangerous." I exhale. "It's hard to explain."

"Try me."

"You wouldn't believe it."

"How do you know unless you try?" She tilts her head with a total smarty-pants expression.

These are the situations that get me in trouble. Here,

Vacation Brain should say, "Keep your mouth shut, dude! You barely know her!"

But Vacation Brain is nowhere to be found. I lean close to her ear and blurt in a whisper, "I have a live T. rex in my room."

Lenora stares at me. "Fine. Don't tell me. For a minute, I thought we could be friends."

I slump. "I knew you wouldn't believe me."

We drive the rest of the torturous fifteen minutes to my house in a deafening silence. Lenora's words clang loudly in my head. *I thought we could be friends.* Clearly, I wasn't thinking at all. I wish I could pull time back like a fishing reel and get a do-over.

Finally Mr. Pickering turns into my driveway. "Here you go, buddy. It was nice meeting you. Next time, stay for dinner." He shakes my hand and winks.

"Thanks, Mr. Pickering," I say, even though I know there probably won't be a next time. Even if there were, considering what happened to Bobbie, I'd probably pass on dinner.

"Nah, call me Ned." He slaps my back. "Walk him to the door, Nora. It's polite."

Lenora slides out of the truck and stands there stiff, her arms crossed, waiting for me to get out. With her dad watching, she follows me to the front door, then says, "Have fun playing with your imaginary dinosaur. See ya."

Her words needle me, and I tug her shirt sleeve as she turns away. I want her to believe me. If she knows I'm telling the truth, maybe she won't be so upset at me.

"Wait. Come inside. I'll prove I'm not lying."

Lenora thinks for a moment, then shrugs and shouts to her dad. "I'm going in for a sec, Dad. Be right back."

He shoots her a thumbs-up.

Once in the house, I do my pet inventory. Check. Both alive and not missing any fur, paws, or tails. "That's Fiddles and Cappuccino," I say, pointing first to the cat, then to the hamster cage. "Do not, under any circumstances, let the cat in my room."

"Whatever." Lenora kneels to scratch Fiddles's chin.

I grab a fistful of deli meat from the fridge, then lead the way down the hall. I open the door to my room slowly. Inside it's the same disaster zone from the day before, but at least my closet door is still closed. *Phew.*

We step inside, and all is quiet. I toss my backpack onto the desk.

"Looks like a normal, disgusting fifth-grade boy's room to me." Lenora raises an eyebrow as she surveys the mess.

I look around too. The heap of spilled baseball cards

stills sits on my dirty laundry pile. I've got filthy socks and a million baseball hats, books, wrappers, and balls on the floor—plus the damage from the T. rex.

"It's disgusting because a Tyrannosaurus rex terrorized it," I say, even though I have to admit, it was pretty disgusting before too.

"You mean that guy?" She points to the rubber version, lying near the equally lifeless toy army men.

I take a deep breath. I'm going to have to open the closet door. I don't want to, but if I'm going to prove Tiny T's existence, I don't have a choice. I cross my fingers and hope he's sleeping. There's no thumping, so it's a good bet.

"Get on the bed and take this." I hold out the butterfly net. Lenora takes it but just stands there. "Up." I point.

Lenora exhales. She smooths the messy covers, and the bed creaks as she crawls on and folds her legs under.

I place my desk chair next to the closet door. Remembering I need to take a picture, I pull my phone out of my backpack. Battery's nearly dead. Shoot. I climb onto the chair and inch the sliding door open.

Nothing happens.

"Okay. I gotta get going," Lenora says, sounding bored. "Dad's waiting."

"No, give it a second!" I slide the door open further

and peer in. Too dark. Leaning in to snatch hold of the light string, I pull down. As soon as the light flicks on, the T. rex barrels out of the closet. Fifty headless plastic army men scramble after him.

"Whoa! Whoa! Whoa!" Lenora yells, holding her hands out in front of her. "What is that!?"

"Told you!" I snap a shot with my phone, just as the battery dies. But I think I got it. "He's a T. rex. I call him Tiny T. Get it?"

The T. rex's nostrils flare, sniffing the salami in my hand, and he butts his thick head against the leg of my chair. I drop some salami on the floor.

"No way!" Lenora comes to the edge of the bed to get a better look. "This is crazy! Where'd you get it? Are we safe? And what are those creepy things?" She points to the army men.

"A zombie army. He bit the heads off my plastic ones." I point to them. "Then the live ones—if you can call them that—came out like that with no heads."

The T. rex swooshes his tail and flings a bunch of the men across the room.

"Came out of where? How can they be *alive*?"

"Came from this." I point to the pouch on my desk. "I found it in Gram's basement. It belonged to my Uncle Marty. It's magic."

"Magic? That's impossible." Her mouth is wide open.

"Clearly not," I say, pointing to the T. rex. "I don't know exactly how it works, but here, it came with this card." I reach over and grab the Madame Zaqar card from my desk.

Lenora reads it. *"The purchased customized enchantment herein, conjured by the eye, is to be activated by one conjurer and passed down by blood.* What does this mean, customized? Who signed this?"

Just then, Tiny T notices Lenora and claws at the bedcovers, trying to climb up.

She tosses the card onto the desk and backs up. "Oh, geez. Will he bite me?"

"He can't climb up the bed."

"You sure?"

"Pretty sure. His arms are too weak. Anyway, that's my Uncle Marty's signature. He must have bought the pouch somewhere. He went to some pretty weird places. I'm not sure how it works, though. It seems to create stuff you think of but only if you're holding it—like my rubber T. rex and these guys, plus this crocodile who ate a turtle from a painting. Only the crocodile went back in by itself, and I can't get any of these guys to do that."

As I speak, Tiny T races back and forth along the bed, looking for a way up. I suddenly realize he's a little less tiny. Actually, way less tiny. His puny arms couldn't reach the covers at all yesterday. Guess keeping him as a pet in a cage is now out of the question.

"He's getting bigger," I say.

"Bigger?" Lenora flattens herself against the wall. "Maybe you should put him back in the closet now!"

"Stay on the bed." I throw a piece of salami to the floor, but Tiny T is more interested in chomping Lenora.

"*Aaaah.* Seriously. Look at those fangs!" Lenora curls into the bed's corner by my pillows. Her knuckles are white around the butterfly net handle.

The T. rex scampers to the foot of the bed, over to my chair, and back again, trying to get one of us. The army men follow, but he kicks them away.

"What are the zombie guys doing?" Lenora asks.

"They're trying to corral him. It's their mission, I guess, because that's what I was thinking when I made them."

"Well, they're not doing a very good job with their mission. Why don't you try un-thinking them away?" Lenora looks like she wants to melt into the wall.

I shrug. "Worth a try, I guess."

"Before he eats me, please!"

I chuck another piece of salami onto the floor, and this time Tiny T notices. He gobbles it up with three quick chomps and lifts his nose to the ceiling to let the last bit slide down his gullet. Then he stretches his tiny T. rex arms out for more, thwacking a squad of army men with his leg.

I grab the pouch off the desk and close my eyes, imagining the T. rex and green guys marching inside. I open them quickly and toss the pouch onto the floor, just as Lenora's dad beeps his horn from the driveway. When I open my eyes again, the creatures are still there.

"It didn't work," I say.

"How am I supposed to get down if you can't get rid of him? Did you read the manual that came with that thing?" She throws my pillow at the T. rex, but he just ducks.

"There was no manual!" I toss a piece of meat closer to the closet, but the dino snarfs it and darts back to get Lenora. "I'm figuring this out as I go. Yesterday I got him into the closet with the deli meat, but he must be onto me now. Try catching him with the butterfly net."

"Me?" she asks. "He's *your* dinosaur. You do it."

"You have the net!"

"Here." She tosses it at me, but it lands on the floor, too far for me to reach.

"Great."

"Let me see that pouch. I'll get him to go in." She leans

over the edge of the bed to reach for the pouch on the floor.

"No!" I swipe it off the floor before she can get it—and before the T. rex can get me. "No one else should touch it until we know how it works."

"You're touching it. Make something that can get rid of him. Like a tank or a superhero or something—not a headless army."

"I didn't *mean* for them to be headless. Of course I'd rather have a superhero." Like one from the *Revengers* movie I watched Sunday with Mom. That would be amazing.

And there it is again. The pouch I'm tightly gripping gets heavy.

"It's happening!" The pouch is bulging now, the sides wriggling back and forth. I fling it onto my desk before whatever is inside eats my hand.

"What if it's bad?" Lenora moves farther into the corner.

We wait, but nothing crawls out. Instead, a lightning bolt—an actual, freaking bolt of lightning—flashes out and fries a black hole in my baseball-shaped rug. Darn, I loved that rug.

Lenora screams.

From out of the pouch, a six-inch high, inhumanly

muscular man crawls out. He's wearing some kind of fur dress tied with a shiny gold belt and waving a large silver mallet.

Lenora's face looks like she just got off a roller coaster—kind of thrilled but also scared and maybe even ready to barf. She backs way up against the wall and away from the hammer-wielding muscle mini-man.

Outside, her dad's horn is sounding longer *beeeeeeeep*s.

The tiny man raises his mallet overhead. Another lightning bolt sizzles a black mark onto my desk next to my backpack. "You requested a hero?"

"What the heck?" asks Lenora.

"I am Thor. Son of Odin, most powerful of all the Aesir!" little muscle man's voice booms. He flexes his biceps then thrusts his hammer high.

"Thor?" Lenora's face scrunches.

I shake my head. Of all the superheroes, this is the one I get?

Thor advances toward Lenora, hammer held high, and jumps from my desk onto my bed. I keep chucking pieces of deli meat at Tiny T while the army continues its single-minded attack.

"Hey! Back off." Lenora holds her hands out. "Don't hit me with that thing." Thor is only six inches high, but that hammer could totally hurt. Her dad's old truck honks again.

Thor lowers the mallet and bows deeply to Lenora. "Never, my lady. I am forever in the service of one as beautiful as yourself."

Lenora's cheeks turn pink, and she smooths her hair.

"You gotta be kiddin' me." I exhale loudly.

Thor whips around, raising his mallet at me. "Are you in danger, my lady, from this giant ogre with the funny dress?"

"Funny dress?" I pull at my shirt. "This is an authentic Red Sox baseball jersey. You're the one with a fur dress."

"This fine hide comes from a two-headed bear I slew with Mjolnir, my mighty hammer." Thor holds it high. "With this, I conquer all giants."

"How about conquering that giant?" Lenora points to Tiny T, who's busy eating the salami I've been pelting. "I'm in danger from that."

"My hammer will destroy this wingless dragon with one single blow!" Thor lumbers over my bedspread toward the edge, mallet raised.

"No, don't kill him!" I cry. I don't want him dead. "Do you know how this magic works? I just want him to go back."

Thor lowers his hammer. "I practice not the art of magic and invocations."

"Can you at least shove him back into the pouch for me, then?"

"Your dragon must return of its own accord," Thor says. "Or by the conjurer's hand."

"I already tried imagining him going back in. It didn't work," I say. "No way I can shove him in with my hand. I'd like to keep it."

"Maybe you have to come up with a spell or something," Lenora suggests.

"A spell?" I shrug and take the pouch from the desk. I close my eyes. "Creatures in my room—*go back where you came from!*"

I throw the pouch on the floor and wait. The T. rex butts his head against my chair. The soldiers try to tackle him. None of them pay attention to my enchantment.

"Nope." Lenora shakes her head.

"How am I supposed to enchant it back in?" I ask.

Thor shakes his tiny head. "Alas, I cannot say."

"How about forcing it back in the closet for now?" I ask. "Along with the plastic army?"

"I do not take orders from ogres." Thor scowls and turns to Lenora. "Is this my lady's wish?"

Lenora's dad has given up on honking and is now

ringing the doorbell like he's sending out Morse code. Lenora nods, and Thor climbs down off the bed. The T. rex lumbers toward Thor, mouth ajar, ready to scoop up a Thor-flavored dinner.

"Watch out!" I holler.

But a swift whack of Thor's hammer across the dinosaur's face almost makes *me* see stars. Thor grabs the T. rex by the leg, holding him one-handed over his head, and marches to the closet, lightning bolts flashing all around. The whole time he's grinning at Lenora. Totally in a show-off kind of way, if you ask me.

Thor deposits Tiny T into the closet and slides the door, leaving it open an inch. "Inside, men!" he orders. The army men snap to attention and file inside. Once everyone is contained, Thor slides the door shut.

"Thank god." I jump off my chair.

"You're welcome!" Thor shouts.

Lenora climbs off the bed. Her dad has added pounding on the front door to his repertoire.

"Be there in a minute, Dad!" she yells.

Thor walks to Lenora's feet and bows again. She kneels down. "You'll stay and help West with . . . his dragon?" she asks.

Thor hoists Lenora's hand up and kisses the back. "As you command. Until we meet again, my lady."

Pretty sure my eyes are doing *the* most giant eye roll ever in the world.

Lenora stands, and her face is all blotchy red. "Uh, I gotta go."

I walk her to the bedroom door, and she gives a tiny, finger-wiggling wave to Thor, who does one last bow, slides the closet door open a crack, and slips in, closing the door behind him.

"Gross. You're flirting with him?"

Her dad is now yelling her name from outside.

"Ha. Jealous?" she asks.

I snort.

"Are you going to keep them?" she asks.

"Dunno. The T. rex is kinda violent, and I'm pretty sure he's growing. So I guess it would be a bad idea to keep him. The little green army would be awesome—if they had heads."

"You should totally keep Thor."

I shrug. "You can have him. What the heck am I going to do with a tiny guy who thinks I'm an ogre?"

"I heard that!" Thor shouts from the closet.

"I'm sure he just has to get to know you. Maybe you could become friends?"

She's a riot. "Sure. *Hey, everybody, this is my new friend—a small mythical god who lives in my closet. In his spare time, he enjoys needlepoint, long walks on the beach, and hammer-clobbering. . . ."*

"Okay, okay." Lenora laughs, then looks serious. "West—you have magic. This is . . . major."

"I gotta figure out how it works, though. I can't keep Mom out of my room forever, and I go to Dad's on Sunday."

Lenora shrugs. "So what's your plan?"

"Tomorrow after school I'm going to see if Gram knows anything—hopefully without letting on that I made a bunch of really dumb, dangerous things using Uncle Marty's magic. Maybe he told her something about it. Maybe she even has the manual."

"Do you think your grandmother will want to talk about him?" she asks. "You said he's missing, right? My mom died a long time ago, and still no one talks about her. People don't like talking about stuff that makes them sad."

I sigh. "I don't want to make Gram sad, but I don't have anyone else to ask." If Pops knew that I took something of Uncle Marty's, then made a dinosaur, then a headless army, then Thor with it . . . man, would I get in trouble. I already get in too much trouble.

"I'll go with you. To your gram's." She tucks her hair behind her ear and looks at the floor. "If you want."

"Really? Sure."

Lenora's face brightens. She puts her hand out to shake mine, which is kind of awkward, but also kind of nice. "Put 'er there, ogre. We'll figure out your magic together."

"Okay." I smile and shake her hand.

She leaves, and I turn to look at the amazing disaster that is my room. I can still smell the burnt wood from the lightning scorch on my desk.

Thump. Thump. Thump. My closet door rattles.

"Fear not, ogre." Thor's muffled shout comes from behind the door. "We shall subdue the mighty dragon!"

I shake my head. Tiny T, a zombie army, Thor, and possibly . . . a new friend.

Not bad for a day's work.

WEDNESDAY MORNING

Thump. Thump. Thump.

"What was that?" Mom looks up from the pan of sizzling breakfast links.

"Nothing." It's a cold October morning, so Mom has turned on the heat. I'm sitting on the kitchen floor in front of the heating vent, sketching while she makes breakfast. This morning I drew the T. rex.

Thump. Thump. Thump.

"There it is again. Is that coming from your room?" Mom steps back from the stove and looks down the hall.

"Nah. Pretty sure it's outside," I lie. "I'll go check."

When I get up, the heat from the wall vent blows my sketch across the floor to Mom's feet. She glances down.

"Great dinosaur drawing, buddy. We could use that one for the school application."

"Or not," I mumble.

"Change your shirt, please!" she calls after me. "I'd rather you didn't wear your Red Sox jersey four days straight."

"I love this shirt." I slide down the hall in my socks.

"I know, and I hate to be the one to break it to you, but you smell funky, hon," she replies as I enter my room.

The thumping is obviously coming from my bedroom closet—like it did *all night long*. Thankfully Mom's room is on the other side of the house and up the stairs.

I put my mouth up to the crack where the sliding closet door meets the wall. "Can you be quiet in there? Mom can hear."

Thump. Thump. Thump.

"Thor. Can't you stop that thumping?" I ask.

"I'm trying, ogre," Thor says. "Your monster is restless this morning. Perhaps if we let him stretch his legs?"

"No way! I don't want him chewing up my room anymore."

"West! Breakfast. On the table!"

"Ogre, I suggest we allow him—and the rest of us—some air and sustenance. I will put him back in the dungeon after. He is no match for my mighty mallet."

"Come on, West! I don't want to be late for work. Again."

"All right. Come on out." I hop onto my bed.

Thor slides the door open a foot and comes out, followed by the green army in formation. Tiny T barrels out of the closet, scattering the plastic army underfoot. I swear he's doubled in size from when he first crawled out of the pouch. His head is now eye level with my desk chair.

"Does he seem . . . bigger today?" I ask.

Before Thor can answer, Tiny T and I notice the same thing—my bedroom door is open. I didn't think to close it when I came in, since I hadn't planned on letting T and the rest out of the closet.

My breath seizes. "The door!"

Too late. Tiny T is way closer to the open door than I am. With no hesitation, he waves his tiny arms and bolts out of the room.

"Shoot!" I grab the butterfly net and rush out the door.

A scaly tail disappears around the corner to the right. He's in the living room. And so is Fiddles, sleeping in her cat bed next to the sofa.

"Fiddles!" I shout, even though Mom might hear. If T notices her, she's in for it. He's bigger than she is now.

"Run, Fiddles, run!" I yell, turning the corner.

"West, please stop playing with the cat and eat your breakfast!"

Fiddles is just lying on her cat bed in the sun, licking her fur, and T hasn't noticed her yet. He's too busy making a beeline for the hamster cage on the coffee table. But then he turns his head and sees Fiddles to his right.

"No!" I run after him, waving the net. "Don't touch her!"

Fiddles doesn't move. She looks up, her lazy eyes glazed. Tiny T detours from his hamster-cage course and heads straight for Fiddles.

I raise the net, yelling, "Watch out, Fiddles! Go!"

Tiny T stands before the cat bed, jaws wide. I jump onto the armchair and try to swoop the net down on him before he gets to Fiddles, but he ducks, and I miss. And what does Fiddles do? She yawns! Then she sticks her paw out, claws extended, and swats Tiny T on the forehead. Her claws get stuck on his head, and he makes a weird T. rex whine, twisting to get free.

I swear Fiddles seems to be smiling. She's either the bravest or laziest cat ever.

Thor and his army, with their short little legs, finally peek around the corner into the room. "Do you need assistance?" Thor asks.

"Get back in my room," I say. The last thing I need is *more* chaos for Mom to notice.

I take one more swipe with the net, then Tiny T finally frees himself from Fiddles's claws and backs away—quickly. I'm ready for him. He runs right into my net—and *doh*—right back out again.

"Darn it!"

Just then, Mom pops her head in from the kitchen. "What are you doing with that net?"

I look at my net, the cat, Mom, then back to the cat.

"Nothing."

T is behind the coffee table, and Thor and the men are tucked around the corner. She must not be able to see any of them or she'd be screaming.

"Leave the cat alone and come eat."

"In a minute."

"Not in a minute, West." Her tone gets all *I'm-the-boss-of-you*. "Now." With that, she disappears back to the kitchen.

Behind the table, Tiny T's dinosaur lips spread, teeth dripping, and in a flash, he's clawing at the hamster cage. Cappuccino runs around her cage, back and forth, trying to get away from T's sharp claws.

"Get away from her!" I swipe the useless net at his head, and he ducks.

"Who are you yelling at?" Mom asks from the kitchen. "You are not using good listening, West. Please don't make me ask again."

I pick up a sofa pillow and throw it at Tiny T, but he just clonks it away with his head.

Thor shouts from his corner at the hallway. "Your ogre-mother is igniting with the anger of a thousand suns."

"Not helpful," I whisper-shout. "I can handle this. Go back to my room."

Tiny T jiggles the cage with his mini dinosaur hands, dodging my jabs.

"It does not appear, ogre, you are handling anything." Thor raises his hammer and marches in T's direction. Tiny T—who has clearly been pelted by Thor like a zillion times by now—takes off, lumbering into the dining room. Right next to the kitchen. Where Mom is.

"Westin Scott, your breakfast is stone cold now. And I'm not heating it back up."

Tiny T's nostrils flare, and he darts toward the dining table, probably lured by the scents coming from my plate of eggs and sausage.

"Sit down and eat now!" Mom's heels click across the kitchen as she walks back toward the living room. Thor and the army are in the center of the room, attempting to make their way to the dining room, where T paws at my unreachable plate.

I throw down the net and grab another pillow, diving headfirst toward Thor, covering him and the army as much as I can. The rest of the army men freeze in place.

Mom pokes her head in. "What are you doing? Playing with your army men? I swear, West."

Thankfully Thor is covered by the flowered sofa pillow, but if Mom looks left into the dining room, she'll see T. I'll be toast.

"What happened to all their little heads?" she asks.

I shrug.

She shakes her head. "Now you don't even have time to eat. Clear your plate and put on your shoes. We have to go." She walks up the stairs to her room.

I run into the dining room, moving as fast as I can in socks, and circle the table so I'm opposite Tiny T. I reach for my plate and bring it down to his eye level, about twenty inches up. "Come here, buddy. Hungry?"

Tiny T spies the plate and charges. I slide across the room and into the kitchen. T follows just behind, nipping at my heels as we exit the kitchen to the hall. I'm finally getting somewhere . . . until Fiddles saunters across our path. Tiny T is startled and makes a detour into the living room to avoid her.

"Shoot!" I zip back into the living room as Mom comes down the stairs. She's going to come face to face with my dinosaur in about one second.

"Hide," I hiss at Thor. He and the men duck behind a laundry basket at the foot of the stairs.

"I'm ready to go, West. Get your things." Mom turns into the kitchen. If she comes into the living room, I'm dead.

I slide the plate of eggs across the floor toward Tiny T. It whizzes past him, under the armchair, and flies to the other side. T chases after it, sticking his pinhead under the chair. His dinosaur butt wiggles behind him, too fat to fit. I grab the butterfly net and try to scoop it over his tail and butt, a pillow at the ready to cover the top.

"Are you trying to capture the cat with that net and a pillow?" Mom is in the room.

I whip around, standing in front of Tiny T, blocking her view. Fiddles has bolted, so Mom doesn't see that the creature trying to get under the sofa is definitely *not* our cat.

"Maybe."

"That's not nice. Put it down, and let's go." She leaves the room.

I run around to the back of the armchair and grab the plate that flung out the other side. "Here, Tiny T. Yummy, eggs. Mmmmm."

Tiny T pulls his head from under the chair and lumbers after me again, arms extended like Frankenstein's monster. I peek around the corner. Mom's head is stuck in the fridge. I motion for Thor to follow.

Moving quickly, I zoom down the hall and cross the threshold to my room, throw the plate toward the closet, and slip behind my door. The plate shatters and the eggs fly off, slamming into my desk as the sausage rolls into the closet.

Tiny T scoots into the room, and after Thor comes in with his army, I close the door. T starts slurping the eggs with a gross sucking sound, then scrabbles into the closet for the sausage.

"Westin! Now! And I mean, now!"

Thor starts heaving the sliding closet door shut. I finish it off so T can't escape.

"Go, ogre," Thor says. "I will subdue your wingless dragon in the dungeon. We will await your return at sundown."

"Thanks. I'll be home late today—going to Gram's after school to try to find out about this magic."

Which reminds me. I grab a fistful of allowance money from my desk drawer to pay Gram back for the sheets I cut.

"Westin. I'm almost out the door."

"I gotta go." I shut the bedroom door behind me and run down the hall. Mom waits by the front door. Her face is tied in a knot, and I brace myself.

"I swear, West. This has to stop. I've been late for work too many times. Where are your shoes?"

"Oh, sorry. They're in my room." I turn, but a tug on my shirt stops me.

"No. If I let you back in your room, you'll never come out." Mom walks to the coat closet. "Put these on." She holds up the brown cowboy boots I got for horse camp last summer.

"Mom, *no!*"

She drops them at my feet. "This is what you get for dilly-dallying, West. I don't know how else I'm supposed to get through to you. Put them on, and let's go."

"But—" I feel the tears build in my eyes. "I'm not wearing those!"

Mom's face is a thundercloud. Any second, horns will jut out of her forehead and fire will shoot out of her ears. Her voice gets really low, and when she does that, I know she means business. "You. Will. Put. These. On. Now."

I make the angriest frown I can and yank the boots from her. I'm wearing basketball shorts again today, of course. They're shiny—clean, even—and navy blue with a white stripe down the side. Josh has the same pair. But nothing, no matter how cool, can make wearing cowboy boots with shorts okay when you're an eleven-year-old boy and there's not a horse in sight.

WEDNESDAY–AT SCHOOL

Some kids whisper to their friends. Others laugh as they pass me. And Nicole, her face twisted in exaggerated disgust, exclaims, "What's wrong with you?"

Snake smirks. "Dude. Nice boots."

Josh doesn't say anything. Probably he just didn't notice.

At lunch, Lenora meets me at my cubby. She looks at my boots and lifts the visor of her baseball cap to smirk at me. "You know, I think Ms. Molly would say this is totally unexpected behavior."

"Not funny. Mom made me wear them."

"Harsh. What'd you do to deserve that?"

"Tiny T got loose this morning. She almost saw. I was

so busy chasing him, I made us too late to even get my sneakers on."

"Bummer." Lenora leans against the wall. "Wanna eat with me?"

Across the quad, Josh and Snake sit down with Alex and Frankie at a small table. If they see me eating with a girl, while wearing cowboy boots . . . ah, no.

"Sorry. I already told the guys I'd eat with them."

Her face falls. "Oh. Okay." She starts to walk away. "So, am I still going to your grandma's with you or what?"

I nod. "Meet at the library. You cool if we walk? Takes like twenty minutes."

"Sure. As long as you walk five feet behind me." She glances down at my boots again, smirking. Then she sighs. "Guess I'll go try to make nice with the Barbie dolls." She heads to the swings where the girls eat lunch.

When I get to the guys' table, no one makes room for me.

"Scoot over, Josh?" I ask.

It's tight, but he'll usually try to make room for me, like yesterday. But today, nothing.

"There's not really room," Josh mumbles.

I pause, waiting to see if he's kidding. He doesn't move. Why's he being like this? It gives me this PB&J-stuck-in-the-throat feeling, and I haven't even started eating.

"What's with the boots?" Frankie can barely contain himself, and I brace for the onslaught of boot jokes.

"He needs 'em to protect his legs from his vicious dinosaur, Frankie. Duh," Alex says as the guys snicker.

"They're for riding the dino around his room," Snake adds through a mouthful of white bread.

They all crack up.

"How would you get the bit in his mouth for the halter?" Frankie pretends to want to know.

"Totally carefully!" Alex gnaws at his own arm like he's getting mauled by a T. rex. The rest of the table howls with laughter.

"He's real!" I say.

"Yeah, really boot-eeful! Ah-ha-ha!" Frankie nearly chokes on his chips as Alex slaps his back.

"Did you bring the picture?" Josh asks.

I sigh. The picture is on my phone. In my backpack. In my room.

"No." I stand there, lunch bag in one hand, sandwich in the other.

"No picture? Hmm . . . I wonder why?" Alex taps his lips and looks skyward.

Josh changes the subject. "Hey, Alex. Frankie says you're blowing up a volcano for the science fair?"

"Can I sit down already?" No one moves.

I look briefly at other tables. It would be weird to eat with kids I don't know. Plus, what would I say if Lenora saw me at another table? I pull out my PB&J and start to eat standing, waiting for one of the guys to scoot aside for me.

"Turd-face, is that what you told him?" Alex swats Frankie's huge noggin.

"That's not what I said. His volcano is going to erupt real lava," Frankie says.

Alex shakes his head. "Dork. Not lava. My volcano shoots up real *fire*."

"Guys? Can you slide over?" I ask again. "I'll bring the picture tomorrow, I swear."

No movement.

"Whoa, *real* fire? They're going to let you do that?" Josh asks.

"I know, right?" Alex nods. "Dad checked it out with the principal. She says it's okay if Dad's there the whole time. The flames shoot up mega high. It's unbelievable."

I stick my knee between Alex and Frankie, nudging Alex to move right. Alex whips a narrow stare at me through his big glasses. "Quit it."

I circle the table, hoping someone will scoot over. As I pass behind Alex, he sticks his leg under the bench behind him, and I trip over his foot. My lunch bag goes flying across the quad, and I land with a thump on my stomach.

Everyone busts out laughing. Snake is holding his sides, doubled over. Even Josh is cracking up.

I pull myself up. My sandwich is smushed all over the front of my shirt. Grape jelly covers the *S* of Red Sox. Peanut butter and bread covers the rest. Snake holds up his phone to get a photo.

I try to laugh along with them, but mostly I feel like crying or screaming or punching someone. "Nice. That was funny, Alex. Gonna go clean it off."

I hurry to the bathroom and spend the rest of lunch trying to wipe off the grape jelly. I only make it worse, and now I have a giant purple-y wet stain on my favorite jersey. It'll probably never come out, and Mom will kill me because authentic baseball jerseys cost like a hundred dollars. She saved up a super-long time to buy this one for my birthday.

In a burst of anger, I kick the metal trash can in the bathroom. It falls over, shooting wet paper towels across the floor, just as Mr. Lowde comes in to do a bathroom check.

"Westin?" he whispers.

"Sorry." I bend down and scoop the gross, wet towels back into the can.

He comes forward to help. "Is everything okay?"

I lift my shoulders, trying hard not to cry.

"Did your parents get my email? I really hope you join the art club, Westin. You have a lot to offer."

I just nod, and I think Mr. Lowde can tell I don't really want to talk because he pats my shoulder like always, smiles, and turns to leave. "I look forward to having you there," he says, surprisingly loudly.

After recess, we have tech class with none other than my un-favorite teacher, Mr. Widelot. We're working on graphics today, so an aide wheels in a media cart stacked with thin, white laptops and starts doling them out to each kid.

Mr. Widelot spies my shirt and makes a face. "You are not getting near a computer with food all over your shirt."

Like his shirt is any better. Today it says:

**MATH TEACHERS AREN'T MEAN.
THEY'RE ABOVE AVERAGE.**

How is that funny? I don't even get it.

"Go get a PE jersey from the gym and put that on instead," he says.

I hang my head. As if my outfit couldn't get any worse. Our PE jerseys are bright orange and have the school mascot—a giant cartoon of a purple bear head—on the front. Plus the gym is on the opposite side of the school, and it smells funny. Like robot farts, if a robot could fart. Which means my PE shirt will smell like robot farts too.

Thanks a lot, Mr. Widelot.

I walk as slowly as I possibly can to the gym and back. When I return to class, Mr. Widelot is at his desk grading papers. I walk in with my humiliating, farty getup—smelly orange PE shirt with the purple bear head, blue basketball shorts, and, of course, cowboy boots.

Everyone else has their faces inches from their laptop screens, but it's not long before the chuckles begin.

At first I figure they're laughing at the way I'm dressed. But when I open my laptop and log on, there's a message waiting in my school inbox. More laughter fills the room.

"Settle down," Mr. Widelot says without looking up. "There should be nothing funny about your graphics project."

But the twitters keep going. I open my inbox. That's weird. The message looks like something *I* sent out to the class. I don't remember doing that. I check the date and time—sent today, thirty seconds ago.

When I click to open the message, I know why everyone's giggling.

"What is everyone finding so funny?" Mr. Widelot

looks up. He walks to Nicole's computer. I'm sure she's looking at the same thing I am.

It's a photo of me. Cowboy boots. Basketball shorts. Red Sox shirt with peanut butter and jelly smeared over it. Only instead of my head, I have a dinosaur head, its jaws snapping open and closed. There's a speech bubble overhead that says, "I'm going to eat Mr. Widelot and fart him out. Watch out for my Wide-farts."

Clearly at least *one* student has gotten super good with the graphics software. I whip my head up. To send this from my account, someone would have to know my password. There's only one person in class who does—Josh.

"Hopper." Mr. Widelot glares at me.

"I didn't—"

"This was sent from your account," he says. "Close your laptop."

"I swear—"

"Come to the front of the room. You can stand by my desk for the rest of class while I get to the bottom of this." Mr. Widelot walks to his desk and sits down. "I expect everyone to delete that photo from their inbox. And I will check."

I slam my laptop closed. I'm so mad that I shove it off my desk. I watch as it tumbles over the edge, realizing too late, as usual, what I've done. I scrunch my eyes closed, hearing the crashing sound of metal and plastic against the floor.

Oh, shoot. Oh, shoot. Oh, shoot. *Brain!*

I crack a lid. Mr. Widelot's eyes are the size of grape-fruits. "You did not just do that. Pick up that laptop and march up here now, Hopper."

My heart is practically beating itself out of my body. Why'd I have to do that?

I grab the laptop and walk to the front of the class with my head hung. There aren't even any *"ooooohs"* this time.

I stand by Mr. Widelot's desk in my colorful outfit and look out at the faces of my classmates. Some are trying not to laugh, a few look impressed, and the girls look mostly disgusted. Snake and Josh won't even look at me. Frankie's sinking way low in his chair, shoulders shaking with laughter. Alex too.

I guess if it wasn't me, I'd think it was funny too.

But it is me.

And I'm not laughing.

"You have lost all class privileges," Mr. Widelot says. "Every tech class, you will work by me at my desk for the entire period." He opens my laptop and hits some keys. "You're lucky it isn't broken."

"But—"

"In total and complete silence. Do you understand?"

I nod, then glance over at Snake. He raises his gaze, just barely, and the corner of his top lip curls up.

And suddenly I get it. Josh didn't do it.

Snake did.

WEDNESDAY—AFTER SCHOOL

I open my fist, and eleven dollars and twenty-seven cents falls onto Gram's yellow kitchen table. The quarter rolls over to the edge, and Lenora catches it as it falls off.

"What's that for, sweetie?" Gram asks. She sets a plate of sugar cookies down in front of us. They're shaped like snowmen, even though it's only October. Lenora grabs one and practically shoves it into her mouth whole.

"For the sheets. Dad said to pay you. It's all I have."

Gram clasps a hand to her chest. "Westin Scott Hopper. You are the sweetest, kindest boy. Even if you have peculiar taste in shoes." She points at my boots, and Lenora laughs.

Hardly anyone calls me sweet and kind. It makes me

feel all warm inside, like sitting next to a campfire with a full bag of marshmallows and a long stick.

Gram takes the cash, grasps my hand, and places the money back in my palm. "As far as your dad needs to know, that debt's been paid. Put the money back in your piggy bank." She takes a teacup from the counter and sets it down on the table, easing herself into the vinyl chair next to Lenora. "So nice to have a visit during the week. You kids are always so busy with soccer and baseball."

She must be thinking of my cousins. Since I was kicked off the baseball team, the only things I'm busy with are video games and an aggressive, prehistoric reptile.

I take a cookie and glance at Lenora. "Gram . . . can I ask you some questions about Uncle Marty? If it's not too sad for you."

At the mention of his name, Gram's eyes water. Lenora was right. And I feel about three inches high for bringing it up.

But instead of shutting me down, Gram says, "Sure. I miss him terribly, but I love to talk about your uncle."

Lenora's eyes go wide. "Really?"

Gram softly pinches my chin. "What do you want to know, sweetie?"

"Where do you think he went?" I ask.

Gram puckers her lips. "Oh, that Marty couldn't sit

still. He probably visited every country known to man. But he didn't say where he was going this time. When I asked, he said, 'Somewhere special. Somewhere I haven't been before.' And that's it. It worries me not to hear from him. He always calls, no matter if he's on a camel in the Sahara or a riverboat in Borneo."

"Didn't he have a job?" Lenora asks.

Gram pushes the plate of cookies to Lenora. "Have another one, dear. Don't be shy. Marty was a curator at the Museum of Antiquities. Then one day, a few years ago, he up and quit. Flew to France and started traveling all over, doing the most adventurous things." She smiles. "He must have saved all his salary, I guess. Started his own collection, instead of curating for the museum, and gathered things from all over the world. What's downstairs isn't even a fraction of it. We had to put the rest in storage."

"Do you think he's okay, Gram?" I ask.

She dabs the corner of her eye with her knuckle. "I know Pops and your dad think something bad's happened." She covers my hand with her own and squeezes. "But I know Marty is on an adventure. A mother knows."

"It's hard when you miss someone." Lenora looks down. "My mom died when I was little. So I know what that's like."

"Oh, dear." Gram pats Lenora's hand now. "I'm so sorry."

They both look like waterworks are just around the corner, so I shovel another cookie into my mouth and wait it out. As I chew, it dawns on me how awful Lenora must feel. When I think about how much I miss Uncle Marty, it's like a giant boulder is trying to lodge itself into the hole he left in my heart. And he's just my uncle. I can't imagine if my mom died when I was little, and I never got to know her. Lenora must feel like she has a meteor-sized hole in her heart.

The oven dings, and Gram sits up. "More cookies." She pushes herself off her chair and shuffles to the oven.

"Did Uncle Marty ever talk about any of his finds?" I ask. "Like the thing I took Sunday? The magic pouch."

Gram laughs as she places the cookies onto a rack. "Oh, your imagination. Just like Marty's. A magic pouch would explain his lifestyle—and how he could afford to be so generous with us. Always trying to pay for things." She sighs.

I can tell she doesn't really believe me. "Gram, I'm serious. He really did have magic."

"I suppose to me, everything he collected was a little strange and magical." Gram sits back down and takes a sip of her tea. "It's a shame he and your father were never close, even as boys." She lowers her chin and sighs again. "Too different."

"There's a manual that supposedly explains the magic." I press on. "Did you guys find anything like that when you were packing up?"

Gram shakes her head, smiling softly. "Can't say that we did. Why don't you go downstairs and take a look around? Maybe you'll find your magic manual."

I raise my eyebrows and instinctively look around for Pops.

Gram leans in and whispers, "It's okay. Pops is out."

"I won't break anything," I say.

She chuckles. "I know you'll be careful. Go on." She waves toward the basement.

I get up and lead Lenora to the basement door. She whispers behind me, "She's really nice." Then she mumbles, "Bet she'd never kill your chicken."

I open the door, then stop. "Don't be scared. It's dark. And there are spiders."

Lenora narrows her eyes. "I live on a farm—not afraid of spiders. Go."

I grope my way down the familiar stairs to the light-bulb string. Lenora is so close her breath steams my neck. Not afraid of spiders, *right*. I pull the switch on.

"Whoa, cool." Lenora walks to an open cardboard

box. "There's so much down here." She holds up an empty soda bottle. "There's one of these in every language. Look, this one's in Chinese."

I immediately go for the taiko drum. It's almost as big as I am and sits on its side on a wooden frame. I pick up the thick drumstick and haul off. *Bang. Boom. Bang bang boom.*

Lenora covers her ears. "West. Cut it out. We need to get serious."

I give the drum a few more whacks, then put the drumstick down. "You look through stuff on this side. Careful of the grenade box." I point to the boxes on our right. "I'll go over here."

"What exactly are we looking for?"

I scratch my cheek. "Something that looks like a manual, I guess. So, look for books or papers?"

Lenora nods and starts unfolding the top of a large box, digging through its contents.

"Oh, and keep your eyes open for an alien hand," I say, opening a dresser drawer.

"A what?" Lenora pulls her hands back quickly.

"Uncle Marty said he had one." I slam the drawer shut. Empty.

"Ew." Lenora picks through his things with her fingertips. "This one's got magician stuff: top hat, wand, cape, and . . . gross." She holds up a taxidermy of a white rabbit.

"*That* is cool." I dig back into a box. "What the heck? This is *nasty.*" I lift some kind of rubbery fish thing with two heads, a horn, bug eyes, and an open jaw filled with red gums and white fangs. "Check it out!"

"Whoa." Lenora's eyes are large. "That's your alien, dude. It's a mummified alien shark."

"It is?" My shoulders fall. "Well, that's disappointing."

"Hopefully, *that* never comes out of your magic pouch." Lenora laughs.

We flip through every book, dig in every container, open every suitcase for what seems like forever. But we find nothing remotely like a manual for a magic pouch.

I slam down the folds of the box I'm searching. "I don't even know what we're looking for." I exhale and sit cross-legged on the cold floor.

Lenora holds up a small wooden box the size of a bread loaf and shakes it. "I wonder what's in here. It won't open."

I sit up. "That's where I found the key to the suitcase."

"What suitcase?"

I jump up and grab the box from her hands. "It had those clothes in it"—I nod to the pile on the floor—"and the magic pouch." I try to pry open the lid, but the box won't budge. I look up, eyes wide as I remember. "There were papers inside!"

Lenora's eyes match mine. "Maybe it's the manual?"

Just then the basement door opens. "Who's down there?" Pops' booming voice barrels down the stairs. "Is that you, Westin?"

I gasp. "Hide the box in your shirt." I thrust it toward Lenora.

She puts her hands up. "Me?"

I push it into her hands. "He won't suspect you."

Lenora groans but tucks the box inside her sweater.

"It's me, Pops. But Gram said I could," I yell up.

"Get up here this minute."

Here we go.

Lenora and I walk up the stairs to find Pops standing with his arms folded in front of his barrel chest. "What have I told you about going down there? Were you in Marty's things? You never listen."

"Pops, I swear, Gram—"

"He's right, he's right." Gram shuffles down the hall from her room. "Leave him alone, Pops. I said he could."

The scowl on Pops's face only grows. "I don't want him in Marty's things. I don't want anyone in Marty's things."

Gram waves her hand in the air as she passes by Pops and goes to the kitchen. "I know, I know. But

Marty wouldn't mind. He loves sharing his things with West, dear."

"That's not the point. . . ." Pops follows her, complaining as they continue arguing in the kitchen.

That's our opening.

"Come on. Let's get out of here." I pull Lenora toward the front door. "Bye, Gram and Pops. Love you!" I shout over my shoulder.

Without looking back, I bolt out the door, again taking something from the basement without Pops knowing. I just hope what I'm taking this time will help solve all the trouble I've made—instead of making more of it.

WEDNESDAY—LATER

On the bus ride home from Gram's, Lenora and I try to pry open the box, but it's sealed like Fort Knox. I curse myself for bumping the combination the other day and cross my fingers that the papers inside are actually the manual. I start my week at Dad's house on Sunday, and I clearly can't take my new zoo with me.

Once home, I immediately kick off my boots, then discover Fiddles slurping from a puddle of milk on the kitchen floor. The fridge door is propped open with a chair, a carton of crushed eggs and crumpled deli meat wrappers sprawled underneath. Bits of leftover spaghetti and meatballs trail down the hall.

"Whoa!" Lenora exclaims.

I run to my room. Plastic army men are in formation at the base of my desk. Thor stands on top, chest puffed out, telling a battle story about some serpent—Jormungander or something—that's going to poison the sky or whatever.

Tiny T bangs against the closet door—*still*. I don't want to know what the inside of my closet looks like. My clothes are probably shredded. I just hope he hasn't touched my Gators jersey. I've been waiting forever to fit into it, and I think this year is the year.

"What happened out there?" I interrupt Thor's story and point toward the kitchen, like Dad does when he's accusing me of something I probably did.

"My lady. Your presence today has brought sunshine into my battle-weary days." Thor bows deeply, and Lenora blushes.

"You could've at least cleaned up after yourself," I continue. "Did you have to leave such a mess?" Wow, those words out of *my* mouth!

Thor scales the desk like it's a cliff and the knobs are his footholds. Then he swaggers over to the closet, a tiny sparkle shining off his toothy grin at Lenora, and nudges open the door. Lenora and I immediately jump up onto the bed.

"What are you doing?" I cry.

Tiny T barrels out of the closet, straight into the center of the room. He's at least a head taller and is close to mid-thigh now—much, *much* bigger than Fiddles.

"I fed your hungry dragon. You see that he grows," Thor says.

"Thank you, Captain Obvious!"

T scrambles over to the bed. His little T. rex head is now able to peek above the edge. He grabs at the bedcovers with his short arms, but they're not strong enough to lift him onto the bed—yet.

"You have to get rid of him, West. Fast. He's going to keep growing," says Lenora.

"You think?!"

Thor wallops Tiny T on the noggin again and drags him back to the closet by his tail. With the coast clear, Lenora and I climb down from the bed and sit cross-legged on the floor. I keep trying combinations on the box, but nothing works.

"Where's the magic pouch?" Lenora suddenly asks.

I point to my sock drawer. "Why?"

Lenora grabs the pouch and the card that came with it. "I have an idea." She sets them on the ground before me. "Hold the pouch and imagine the box open. But you can't think of anything else. No race cars or video games."

I bang a fist against my forehead. "I *wasn't* thinking of those things. Now that's *all* I can think of. I shouldn't go anywhere near that pouch!"

Her lip curls down. "Sorry. Want me to try?"

I shrug.

Lenora lifts the pouch and closes her eyes, palms extended out in front of her. I hold my breath. After a moment, she opens her eyes. I try the lid. Still locked.

"Darn," she says.

I reach for the Madame Zaqar card on the floor. There must be some clue here. "Wait. The card says, *The purchased customized enchantment herein, conjured by the eye, is to be activated by* one *conjurer and passed down by blood. Purchaser hereby agrees to all terms* . . . blah blah blah."

I look up.

"*One* conjurer?" Lenora repeats.

"Passed down by blood," I say. "*I'm* Uncle Marty's blood. *I'm* the one conjurer now." I slump. "This is terrible."

Thor shrugs. "I must concur."

"Why is that so bad? Who wouldn't want magic that only works for them?" Lenora asks.

"Because if it works for only me, maybe Uncle Marty really is dead," I say.

Lenora's eyebrows inch together. "Oh." She places a hand on my shoulder. "I'm sorry."

I inhale as that sinks in, wondering if there could be some flaw in the logic, some way it doesn't mean Uncle Marty is really gone forever.

Lenora turns to Thor. "This magic must come from the same place you do. Are you sure you don't know anything?"

Thor waves his arm dramatically. "My lady, the place I come from is the Other Realm. It is where the stars meet the imagination, where time drifts on a river of tears and joy and thoughts and dreams. It is everything, and it is nothing. It is now, and it is never." He lifts his mallet high. "There is magic, aye, both good and bad. What I know is that one must be wary of dark magic and the temptation it summons. It is best avoided."

"Generally vague and mostly unhelpful," I mutter under my breath.

"What about what it says on the card? *Customized enchantment.* Any idea what that means?" Lenora asks.

"I am sorry, no. Brute strength is all I require to make wishes come true. If it were me, I would single-handedly subdue your dragon and escort him back to the Other Realm." Thor slashes his mallet through the air and stops. "Alas, ogre, you lack the necessary musculature for such strength, and I cannot do it for you."

"Super helpful observation." I sigh.

"You conjured forth," Thor continues. "You alone must conjure the return."

"I wish I'd conjured forth a Thor that talked normally," I say.

Lenora thrusts the pouch toward me. "You just have to focus."

I wave the pouch away. "Maybe we haven't met. My name's Westin Hopper, otherwise known as Hyper Hopper. Thoughts faster than a speeding rubber band, able to conjure a T. rex in a single bound . . . Anyway, I don't know the spells or whatever."

"You have to try. Hold the pouch and think of the box opening," Lenora insists. "I'll hold onto it until you're focused. My mom was a yoga teacher, so I can help you be mindful." She adjusts herself to face me.

"I thought your mom was a dancer who did MMA," I say.

"Don't change the subject." Her kneecaps touch mine, just the tiniest bit, and mine bounce, as usual. She taps one to make me stop. "Close your eyes and take in a deep breath."

I breathe all the way to the bottom of my lungs . . . and bounce my knee.

"Count to four and let it out. One, two, three, four." She exhales. "And quit bouncing your knee."

I crinkle my nose and force myself to stop bouncing. It's super hard. I start tapping my fingers on my thighs instead.

Lenora reaches over and puts her hand on mine. "Shh. Breathe in . . . and out. Relax."

I'm supposed to relax with a girl's hand on mine?

"Now focus on the box. The lid is open."

Box. Lid. Open. Breathe in. Breathe out. Don't bounce. I chew my bottom lip.

"Do you see the open box in your mind?"

I nod.

"Good. Now just keep picturing that." Lenora's knees press harder into mine, and I feel her setting the scratchy velvet pouch on my leg. She places my hand on top of the pouch.

I imagine the open box. I'm a conjurer now. I can do magic—maybe all sorts of magic. Like flying and becoming invisible. I could seriously mess with Mr. Widelot if I were invisible. Maybe I'll become a famous wizard, and they'll make a bunch of movies about me, and I'll go to wizard school instead of nature school or whatever, and I'll get a wand and ooh, cool, my own owl and a flying broo—

My eyes fly open, and I throw the pouch off me.

"What?" Lenora looks at it.

"I was doing great. But then . . ."

"Uh-oh."

And there it is. Another lump. It thrashes inside the pouch.

"My mind wandered! To wizards and owls and flying brooms and . . ."

"You didn't." Lenora reaches for the pouch and slowly unties it. A bird flies out, white and round with large dark eyes. "It's an owl!" she exclaims.

The owl is tiny, about the size of a hummingbird, but definitely an owl. It flies in circles before landing on the bookshelf, where it tucks its wide wings to its sides and blinks its heavy eyelids twice.

I check the box. Still locked. "Darn it." So not only did I *not* conjure the box open, but also, of all the cool things I pictured, I got the owl.

Lenora stands to inspect our winged guest. She turns to Thor. "Can we keep it?"

Thor swings his mallet once, then poses with a knee bent, warrior-style. "That is betwixt the conjurer, the will of the raptor, and the Other Realm."

Lenora strokes the tiny owl's feathers. "I guess it's harder for you to focus than I realized." She holds her finger out like a perch and smiles when the tiny owl mounts it. "And you're right, you shouldn't be anywhere near this pouch with your mind." She reaches down and picks up the pouch. "What do we do now?"

As soon as Lenora sets the pouch on my desk, the owl takes flight off her finger and swoops right into the opening. In an instant, it disappears.

"Darn." Lenora frowns.

"Really? The owl flies back in?" I exclaim. "Just like that?"

Thor strikes a new pose, mallet overhead, other hand out straight. "This raptor was likely displeased with the foul odor of your chamber."

I stand up and start toward the door. "I have an idea. I'll be right back." I run to the garage and return with a large screwdriver and heavy hammer. "Hold the box on its side," I tell Lenora.

She puts the box between her knees. I kneel and position the screwdriver against the crack between the lid and base. With all my brute force, I slam the hammer down. The lock snaps more easily than I expected, and I fall forward. The screwdriver slips off the box and jabs down hard.

Lenora gasps, and her eyes go wide. The screwdriver is sticking into my carpet, an inch from her leg.

Thor leaps off the desk and runs over, mallet circling. "My lady! Has the ogre injured you?"

Lenora raises her hands. "All good." She glances at me. "But maybe we let Thor do the hammering from now on?" She looks at the now-open box. Inside are the rolled papers I saw when I first found the key. "Well, you did it."

I dive in and unroll the papers.

"Is it the manual?" she asks.

I shake my head. "Looks like drawings." I hold them up. "This one's a car . . . this one looks like weird money. A drawing of an airplane ticket from San Francisco to Paris for a Martin Q. Hopper."

"Let me see." She lifts a few drawings to inspect them.

"I think Uncle Marty drew these," I say. "I remember when he got this Mustang. Dad was so jealous. And I think this is supposed to be the money they use in Europe—Euros. Uncle Marty gave me some once."

"Hmm. He's a good artist." Lenora says. "But why would he bother saving all these drawings? I mean, they're not *that* good."

I don't have an answer for that. We look through the rest of the papers. All drawings, no instructions, no manual. Not one thing that explains the magic.

"Well, this was a giant waste of time." I slam the box cover down.

Lenora puts her hand on her hip. "Not entirely, grumpy. We now know the magic only works for you.

And that we should keep you away from it or we could wind up with tiny King Kong or Dracula by mistake."

I rub my face in my hands. "Why won't the T. rex just go back, like the owl and the crocodile?"

"We may never know why your dragon remains," Thor says. "Perhaps he has an affection for this world. Perhaps the Other Realm sent him to tutor such an inept ogre-turned-conjurer."

I shake my head. "I can't even understand you half the time."

"I think he means Tiny T could be here to teach you something," Lenora says.

"Ha!" I burst out. "Here's what I've learned so far: I have to get rid of him or he's going to eat me."

"Fear not, ogre. I shall not let harm befall a servant of my lady." Thor raises his mallet.

I give him a weak smile. "Thanks." He's strong for a tiny dude, but my growing prehistoric problem will gobble him up before long. Followed by me for dessert.

Just then a horn beeps in the driveway.

"Must be my dad," Lenora says. "I should go before he tries to break down the door again."

I nod. "Mom will be home any minute. She'll freak if she sees the mess by the fridge. I'd better go clean it."

Using a drumstick from a toy drum I broke eons ago,

I lift the magic pouch off the floor. Then I open the wooden box with the drawings and slip the pouch inside. I tuck the box in my sock drawer for safekeeping.

Lenora stands. "Now what?"

"No idea," I say. The closet door shakes as my dinosaur thumps it from inside. "Tiny T is growing fast. This is getting scary."

"Maybe it's time to tell your mom?" Lenora suggests. "If my mom were alive, that's what I'd do. She'd know how to fix it."

Maybe her mom would. But I don't think even my super-duper helicopter Mom would know how to repair this magic gone wrong. I'm going to have to fix this trouble myself.

WEDNESDAY NIGHT

I'm in the middle of researching magic on the internet when there's a knock on my door. "West? Time for bed," Mom says from the hall.

"Don't come in!" I bolt to my door, open it a crack, and slip out to her in the hallway.

"I thought you'd be done organizing by now," Mom says, trying to peer around me. "Can I peek in?"

I block her path. "Nope. No way. You promised, remember?" Even in the dim light of the hall, I can see that Mom's eyes are sort of red and puffy, like she's been crying. This can't be good. When Mom cries, it's usually because of one of the "D" words.

Detention.

Dad.

Divorce.

And disorder. When the doctor told Mom I had ADHD, she cried. She tried to hide it from me, but I totally knew. Can't say I blame her. My life would be completely different—and way easier—if I could focus, sit still, and remember stuff.

My insides tense. "Am I in trouble?" *Mr. Widelot.* It was just a matter of time. He probably ratted on me for not showing up to detention three days in a row. He still hasn't said anything in class. He's deliberately messing with me.

Mom makes a funny face. "Did you do something to get in trouble? If so, best to come clean now."

I look down and kick the floor with my heel. "You might be getting a call from Mr. Widelot." I look up. "But I don't think sticking a tongue out at Nicole should have gotten me in trouble. I mean, geez, big deal. Plus, I have ADHD—it makes me do stuff!"

Mom shakes her head. "Sometimes I think we never should've told you that you have ADHD. You can't use it to excuse your behavior." She raises a finger. "It's an explanation, not an excuse. And it doesn't mean something's wrong with you, got it? You're perfect the way you are."

"Uh-huh." Like I buy that.

"I'll deal with your teacher if he calls." She pulls me in for a hug. "Sometimes people only see the negative stuff. But your mind operates in amazing ways. Like your terrific imagination and your drawings."

Okay, now she's hallucinating. Next she'll tell me I can leap tall buildings and catch speeding bullets. If my mind is so "amazing," why do my grades reek? Oh, and then there's that bit about the *creatures in my room* that I conjured while Brain was dancing the hula. Amazing, my butt.

"So why were you crying then? Is it Dad?"

Mom inhales, kind of ragged-like, and I think she might start tearing up. "It's grown-up stuff. You let me worry about it." She chews her lip.

Guess that settles it. Dad's the D word.

Suddenly Mom's rotor blades fire up again. "Maybe tomorrow we can work on your charter school application. We need to start on that essay. Oh, and how was your playdate at that girl's house?" She squeezes my shoulder. "Is she nice? Does she want to come over for dinner? You thanked her folks, right?"

I can practically feel the downdraft as the helicopter whirs.

"It wasn't a playdate, Mom. It was fine. She's okay."

Minimal info is the key.

"That's all I get, huh? 'Fine' and 'okay'?"

"I guess."

"Well, sweet dreams, then. Don't forget to call your dad to say good night." Mom kisses my forehead. "We're going to be okay, you and me. We are. I love you so much." When she pulls away, her eyes are shiny with tears again.

I think about what Lenora said—that maybe Mom could fix the prehistoric trouble in my closet. But as she drags a fingertip under one eye, I decide the last thing Mom needs is another *D* word on her list—*dinosaur* would be a big one.

Back in my room, I phone Dad to say good night.

"Hey, squirt, did your mom get my email about the private school?" Dad asks as soon as he picks up. "I need you to start filling out the application, and we'll need a letter of recommendation from a teacher. Who would be good to ask?"

Er . . . no one? Sometimes Dad is a little out of touch with my academic reality.

"I'll think about it," I say instead.

"Just calling to say good night?" he asks. "I'm in the middle of a brief I need to file." That's lawyer-speak for "I can't talk to you right now."

"Oh. Yeah, that's all," I reply. "Sorry."

"No, that's okay, buddy. I have a minute," he says. "How was your day?"

"Been better." Like the days I didn't have to wear cowboy boots and basketball shorts to school and keep a man-eating prehistoric lizard from devouring my face. For starters.

"Pops called me," Dad says. "You went into the basement with some girl?"

"Gram said I could!" My voice gets high.

"West, you know Pops doesn't want you in Marty's things. You didn't take anything, did you?"

"No." The lie just jumps right out of my mouth before I can stop it. "I mean, sort of. But Gram said I could take it."

"Westin."

"The thing I took is magic, Dad. Real magic." Again, blurting without thinking. Vacation Brain is on a roll tonight. But maybe it's okay. Maybe Dad could help. "And these things appeared, dangerous things, and I can't get rid of them."

Dad exhales, and I can practically feel his breath through the phone. "Buddy, I know you have a great imagination, but now's *not* the time. I'm in the middle of this major case. Let's talk about this on Sunday. And about taking things that don't belong to you."

"But, Dad—"

"Sunday, Westin. Okay?"

"Please, Dad? Please?"

"I'm not going to say it again. Final."

I pout silently.

"Stop pouting. I'll see you this weekend. Good night."

Without another word, Dad hangs up. Dang it. Just like I thought, I'll have to tackle this trouble alone—and fast—before my life blows up completely.

THURSDAY MORNING

"Are you going through some kind of growth spurt, sweetie?" Mom is fixing me another PB&J sandwich because there's basically no other food left in the house. Tiny T has eaten it all. "I bought two pounds of deli meat on Monday and had to get more yesterday."

"Guess so." I'm too busy shoveling scrambled eggs onto toast for the dinosaur in my closet to say more. I take a few bites for myself. I'd rather have frosted cereal, but Mom says she read somewhere that protein is good for my wandering brain. I wish she'd stop reading.

Thump. Thump. Thump.

"There's that noise again." Mom puts down the knife and heads toward the hall to investigate.

"No, I'll go!" I jump up. "I have to get my shoes on anyway."

"Did you put your homework in your backpack? Don't forget to brush your teeth!" she calls after me.

"Okay!" I remember to shut my bedroom door behind me this time. Then I carefully crack the closet door a few inches. Thor squeezes through the opening, and I quickly close it behind him. He's taller now, almost a foot high. Apparently the only things *not* growing are the plastic army men and me.

"Good morning, fine ogre. Tell me, what news of the kingdom today?"

"For the millionth time, I'm not an ogre." I kneel down and offer my palm. "Eggs, toast, and bacon. Take some, and give the rest to T. How's it going in there?"

"Your dragon continues to increase in size, but we control him well. He is weak and hungry and bruised from my prowess with the hammer. He has, however, clawed through most of the fine drapery in this dark hall in his search for sustenance."

"Fine drapery?"

"The large swaths of material hanging from up above."

"Oh. My clothes. Great."

"Have you found the way to send him home, ogre?"

Thor takes a tiny mouthful of eggs, followed by a small bite of bacon.

"Not yet. I have to get to school, so there's not much I can do about it right now." I peer into my backpack to double-check that my phone is inside. "Today I need to prove to my friends that I'm telling the truth about the T. rex."

I reach into my drawer for the wooden box, push aside Uncle Marty's drawings, and slip the box into my backpack. "And just in case they don't believe me, I'm bringing the pouch. That will prove I have magic."

"Ogre, it is not for me to judge in matters of giants. But might I suggest this is not a good plan?"

I shake my head. "You don't get it. They don't want to hang out with me because of one silly, tiny mistake I made. All that will change when they realize I really do have magic."

"If one mistake loses a friend, and a treasure gains him back, a true friend he never was indeed."

"Yeah, yeah, whatever, Yoda. Try speaking English next time." I stand.

"I am merely attempting to assist my lady's pig-headed ogre."

I sigh. "You're right, I'm sorry. You are helping. And I know you probably want to get back to . . . Other wherever. Are you cool to hang for a while, at least until I figure out how to get rid of Tiny T?"

Thor cocks his little head to the side. "'Cool to hang'?"

"Yeah, I mean, will you stay a little longer?"

"The headless green warriors and I can contain the giant dragon in your chamber until my lady gives command that I am no longer needed. Until then, I am at your service, ogre."

I have to laugh. Do I really look like an ogre to him? "Thanks. I mean it."

"Westin, are you ready?" Mom calls from the kitchen. "Did you figure out what that noise was?"

"Nothing!" I holler back and reopen the closet door a crack. "I gotta go."

"Thank you for the sustenance. Go forth, and may the strength of Odin be with you." Thor hefts the piece of toast with the remaining eggs and bacon over his head and sneaks back into the closet.

I'll take all the help I can get from Odin if it means figuring out how to send these creatures back to wherever they came from and out of my life.

THURSDAY—AT SCHOOL

Mom drops me curbside at school—late as usual—so I get a late slip from the office. Everyone is already lining up by the buses for our field trip to the museum. The entire fifth grade is going because we're studying Egypt, and we all have to write some long, boring report on an Egyptian topic.

I'm dreading it, because I rot at organizing long projects. But I guess the Egyptian stuff is pretty cool. Pharaohs and mummies and pyramids.

I scout around for Josh and see him lining up at the first bus with Snake, Alex, and Frankie.

"Josh!" I run toward him, pulling my phone out of my backpack. "I have the picture. Look!"

"No cutting in line," Snake says.

"I'm not cutting. I have the picture of the T. rex." I hold my phone out for them to see, but Mr. Widelot appears before they can get a good look. His shirt today reads:

THERE ARE 3 KINDS OF PEOPLE IN THE WORLD: THOSE WHO ARE GOOD AT MATH AND THOSE WHO AREN'T.

"Back of the line, Hopper," Mr. Widelot says. "No phones at school."

"But—"

"Go." He ushers me away.

I take my place at the end of the line. A moment later, Lenora walks up with Alicia and a couple of other girls.

". . . you can get them at the mall. Everyone is wearing them," Alicia is saying. "It would look totally cute on you. Instead of . . ." She gives Lenora a once-over. ". . . you know."

Lenora tilts her head, smiling a fake smile. "Sweet. Thanks for that. Gotta go." She turns her back on the girls and faces me. "So, what's the plan? Did you tell your mom?"

I shake my head. "No. She has enough going on. I tried to tell my dad, though, and he totally blew me off. So I have no plan. Nada. Zip." Nothing except proving to the guys that I'm not lying.

"Want to sit together on the bus?" she asks.

I look over at Josh. "Um . . ."

Lenora sees where I'm looking and elbows me in the side. "If we're going to be friends, you can't care what those cretins think about it."

"They're not cretins." She doesn't get it.

"If you say so," she grumbles.

When it's time to load the bus, Lenora gets on first and plops down in a window seat halfway up. I stand in the aisle by her row. Josh and the rest of the guys are sitting in the way back.

"West, sit down already." Lenora pats the seat next to her.

I slip quickly into the seat. I try not to let my knobby knees touch hers, which means I'm sitting so close to the edge of the seat, I might as well be in the aisle.

Mr. Widelot claps at the front of the bus to get our attention. "Settle down, eyes front," he says. "We're going to be on this ride together for one hour. I expect behavior representative of Mistral Mill students. No monkey business."

I tap my fingers on my thighs, bouncing my knees too. An hour is a long time for me to sit in one place with Mr. Widelot waiting to pounce.

"So . . . what are our next steps?" Lenora asks after Mr. Widelot takes his seat.

I shake my head. "I dunno. Last night I did an internet search on magic to see if I could find anything out."

"And?"

I lift my shoulders. "Nothing about a magic pouch or a Madame Zaqar. But it seems like there's white magic and dark magic. White magic is good. Dark magic is for evil or selfish purposes. I've probably already done dark magic a million times. A raging T. rex in your room is pretty dark."

"Aw, give yourself a break," Lenora says. "I bet dark magic is doing bad things on purpose. Like imagining someone's nose falling off. Or their hair turning purple forever. You know, because you hate them."

I picture Cranky Steve with purple hair and no nose. I see the temptation.

"Uncle Marty signed that card saying he'd never use the magic to do harm. We probably should make our own sort of code for it."

"What do you mean, a code?" Lenora asks.

"We need rules, so I'm not tempted to do something bad with it, like Thor said. Like what if one day I lose it on Mr. Widelot and decide to create a giant robot that smashes his house?"

Lenora twists her lips. "I suppose."

"There must be a way to control the magic. And once

I figure it out, who knows what my brain might do. That's why I need a code. The first rule is that I won't ever touch the pouch unless I clear it with you first."

Lenora shrugs. "Deal. But once you learn to control the magic, what *are* you going to do with it? You know, that isn't dark?"

"I haven't thought that far ahead yet." But that gives me an idea. "Maybe I could make something for you!"

"Me? Really?"

"Sure. After all, you're helping me. What can I bring to life for you?"

Lenora wrinkles her forehead. "I don't know. I'll have to think. What would *you* wish for? Other than a flesh-eating reptile."

"Aren't you hilarious." I think about Mom last night, how sad she seemed. How we might have to move. "Money, I guess." Then it hits me. "Wait, no. A new brain. A good one."

"What are you talking about?" Lenora asks. "What's wrong with your brain?"

"This one has ruined my life. It makes me annoying, makes me say things without thinking, doesn't stop me from spacing out and missing passes. All my friends are mad at me because of it."

Lenora looks at me. "Geez, West. *All* your friends?"

I pause, then hit myself on the head. "See? That's exactly what I mean. A better brain wouldn't have let me say that."

She shakes her head. "You don't need a better brain, silly. You just need to stop being so hard on yourself."

We fall silent for a while. This is going to be a long ride, so I pull out my sketchpad and pencils.

"What are you doing?" Lenora asks.

"What's it look like?" I ask, pulling out a colored pencil.

"You draw?" she exclaims. "Are you any good?"

I shrug.

"My mom was a good artist," she says.

Of *course* she was. Seems like Lenora's mom has done everything there is to do in the world. Which is good, I guess, seeing as how she left it early.

I side-eye Lenora. I wonder what that would be like. Not to remember my mom. To only have a dad and a mean grannie.

I think it would rot.

"Will you draw me something?" she asks.

I scrunch my lips. I don't usually do that. Someone might ask for flowers or a rainbow or baby unicorns.

"Depends," I reply. "What do you want?"

Lenora crinkles her nose. "How about . . . a woman holding a little girl's hand?"

My point exactly. "Can they be running from a giant man-eating alien shark?"

She taps her fingers to her lips. "Well . . . I guess that's okay."

So I start drawing.

Occasionally Lenora points out the window at a cool car or asks me stuff like what other pets I've had or if I've ever been to Disneyland. Mostly I draw, and she stares out the window as the bus rushes down the highway. Every now and then, the bus jolts, and I slam into her.

Awkward.

After a while, I realize Lenora is watching me. I can feel her gaze, which is weird because no one has ever stared at me while I draw. But in this case, I guess I don't mind the attention.

"You're freaky focused while you draw. Like, you're not moving or bouncing or anything," Lenora says.

I lift my pencil from the paper. "Yeah. Because I like it. I'm deciding what color to use, what shape to put where. Whether the eyes should be bigger or farther apart. I can stay really focused when I draw."

"Huh. Who knew?"

I go back to drawing. When I finish, I tear the sheet out and hand it to her. "Here."

"Whoa. West, you're even better than your uncle!"

Lenora's mouth hangs open. "The girl totally looks like me—like that's my nose and my exact hair color." She points. "And how did you remember all those details from the alien shark?" She looks at me like we're meeting for the first time. "Can I keep it?"

I shrug. "If you want." I put my drawing stuff away, but after a few minutes of nothing to do, I start to get bored.

"Doo-do-dooo. Doo-do-dooo," I say under my breath, tapping my knee. "Doo-do-dooo." I add a bouncing leg. "Doo-do-dooo." This goes on for a few minutes while my mind pings around, bored.

Lenora reaches down and squeezes my knee tightly. "You have to stop!"

"What?"

"The bouncing. The doo-do-doo-ing. Can't you just sit still?"

Here we go. I'm driving her crazy. Like I drive everyone crazy, apparently. Probably should have kept drawing.

"Sorry."

"Don't say sorry. Just stop," she says.

"Okay. But it's just going to start up again in like two seconds. I can't make it stop."

"Of course you can. That's nuts."

I inhale and look away. "You don't understand."

"What's not to understand?"

"Vacation Brain. It doesn't let me stop, which is why I'd like a better one. It's like if I can't bounce my knee or make a noise, a rumbling pit of lava will explode out of my mouth, eyes, and ears."

"Wow." Lenora pauses, then taps my knee. "You can bounce it then. I don't mind."

I tilt my head back and raise a brow. "Really?"

"Yeah. I don't want lava all over my shoes." She smiles. "I'll bounce with you." She slams her sneakers into the bus floor like she's running in place. "Come on."

She slaps my knee, and I join in her thumping. No one's ever *let* me bounce my knee. Or joined me. Not even Mom.

The kids sitting in front of us whip around and dart an evil look. "Quit it," one of them hisses.

Lenora and I explode into giggles and slink down in our seats. I can't believe Friendship Group actually worked for once. Lenora is fun.

I sit back up and something hits the back of my cap. "What the?" A piece of popcorn lands in the aisle by my feet. Then another hits my neck.

I turn around. "Who's doing that?"

Snake and Alex are in the last row, looking out the window, and Josh is reading a comic book, but they all are trying hard to stifle grins.

I face forward again, but a moment later, popcorn hits Lenora's ear. "Hey!" she exclaims.

Then come the whispers.

Someone starts low with *"West and Lenora, sitting in a tree"* in a sing-songy voice. Unmistakably Frankie's.

Then Alex chimes in. "Hey, Lenora. Has he hit you in the face with a basketball yet?" he calls.

This brings the back of the bus to its knees. Mr. Widelot doesn't even turn around to shush them. He's probably listening to an algebra podcast.

Lenora's cheeks darken, and her lower lip curls.

I spin around in my seat. "Not funny, Alex. And I didn't hit Snake in the face."

"Settle down back there!" Mr. Widelot hollers with a pinched face. "Hopper, face forward." Oh, sure, now he turns around.

I slump back down. "Sorry," I whisper to Lenora.

She just shrugs it off. "Not cretins, huh?"

We're silent again for a while. I bounce my knee some more.

And she just lets me.

THURSDAY—AT THE MUSEUM

Lenora and I file into the museum behind our classmates. The tour guide gathers everyone, all eighty of us, in a big room, and, in a squeaky voice that echoes off the walls, explains what we're about to see and what the rules are.

I'm standing in the back by this freaky-looking mummy. He's all wrapped up in dirty bandages, except for the lower half of his face, and his gray teeth stick out of his rotting gums in a wide, fleshy smile. He's totally creeping me out, so I nudge Lenora to move to the right, where there's more air.

". . . artifacts are on display. But even though they're not behind glass . . ." the tour guide drones.

Josh is clear on the other side of the group. I'll have to make my way over to him once we start walking so I can finally show him the T. rex picture.

". . . over the rails or touch in any way, you will set off the alarm. Everyone got it?" the tour guide asks.

Everyone nods, including me, even though I have no idea what she said. Which is seriously a shame because two seconds later I lean back on the railing, and piercing alarm bells go off.

Everyone jumps, and Mr. Widelot is on me like a shot.

"Hopper!" He grabs my arm and pulls me away from the exhibit.

"What'd I do?"

Lenora's hands fly to her ears to block the sound, and she looks like she's about to burst with laughter. She manages to hold it in, but no one else does. My cheeks burn with embarrassment.

"You did exactly what our tour guide just said not to do." Mr. Widelot's head looks like a dodge ball about to explode as he points to the large sign hanging on the railing, right where I was standing.

CAUTION: SENSITIVE ALARM. DO NOT LEAN OVER RAILING.

"If you were paying attention, you'd know that," he hisses.

"Oh. Sorry."

Betting he wishes I had forgotten that permission slip right about now.

After a security guard checks to make sure I didn't swipe any ancient artifacts, the alarm finally stops ringing. Everyone turns to follow the tour guide to the first exhibit.

I manage to stay mostly out of trouble for the rest of the morning. But every time I have an opening to get to Josh, Lenora pulls me toward some freaky object, or Snake moves in on Josh with a joke or something. I'm beginning to feel like a stalker.

At lunchtime, we're directed to picnic tables in a shaded area outside the museum. Lenora grabs a spot at a table where Evan and Marjorie from Friendship Group are sitting. I stand there holding my lunch bag. A few feet away, Josh and Snake sit down at the base of an oak tree. There's plenty of room to sit near them.

I tap my heel against the pebbly ground. "Um. I'll be right back," I tell Lenora, inching toward the guys.

"Where are you going?" she asks.

I don't answer.

"Oh, great," Snake says as I approach.

I plop down on the dirt next to Josh. "Hey. I have the T. rex photo." I pull my phone out of my backpack and turn it on. I spy around the yard to make sure no teachers, especially Mr. Widelot, can see.

"Really?" Josh asks, taking a bite from his sandwich.

My phone powers up, and I flick to my photos. I only have one shot—the one I took just before my phone died. It's a little blurry, but you can totally tell that it's a T. rex.

"Here, see? That's my room. And that's a T. rex." I point to the screen.

Josh takes the phone from my hand and brings it closer to his face. "Let me see." He pinches outward to enlarge the photo. "Hmmm."

"I told you. A T. rex."

"What's it doing?"

"Coming out of my closet. That's where I keep it. Otherwise it attacks."

"Gimme that." Snake leans in and takes the phone from Josh. "Don't be dense. That's fake."

"It's not fake," I say. "I swear."

"It is kind of blurry," Josh says.

"I would've taken a video, but my battery died," I explain.

"That's a plastic T. rex," Snake insists.

"It's not plastic. It's blurry because it moved. Could a *fake* T. rex move?"

Josh shrugs.

Snake makes a face. "No, but you know what else can't move? *Any* T. rex. Because they don't exist anymore. Anywhere." He chucks the phone straight at my face, and I barely manage to catch it before it hits me in the eye.

"Hey, watch it," I say. "Come over, Josh. See for yourself."

Josh scrapes at the dirt with the side of his shoe. "No, man. Can't. Basketball." He shoves another bite into his mouth and nods his chin at Alex, who's waving them over. "Alex wants us to sit over there at that table."

Without another word, he and Snake get up and turn away from me.

"Wait. I'll prove it." I reach into my backpack and pull out the wooden box, opening the lid to reveal the red pouch inside. "I brought the magic pouch I used to make the T. rex. I can make anything you want. Anything!"

That gets their attention.

Snake hits Josh on the arm and smirks. "Gee, Hyper, like what? Can you make yourself disappear?"

Josh actually laughs at that, which stabs my heart a little.

I ignore Snake. "I'll make something for you, Josh."

Josh shrugs. "I dunno." But then Snake whispers in his ear, and Josh says, "Make a three-headed tree frog?"

"Okay!" I put my hand into the box, on top of the

pouch, and think of a three-headed tree frog. This is going to be so cool. The guys are going to die when they see it.

I pop open my eyes and pull out the pouch. It's empty. I squint in frustration. What the heck?

"I figured." Snake pulls on Josh's shirt. "He's a fake. Let's go."

They turn and leave. I feel like throwing the pouch on the ground. Why didn't it work this time? I shove the wooden box into my backpack, then drag myself back to the table where Lenora sits. I drop my stuff on the ground and throw myself onto the bench.

"What are you doing, West?" Lenora leans over the table and whispers, so Evan and Marjorie can't hear. "Did you just try to make something for them? What about the code we *just* came up with? That you wouldn't touch the pouch without asking me first? That was *your* idea."

I shrug and look at the ground. "They wouldn't believe me, so I panicked. It didn't work, anyway."

"Who cares if those dipwads believe you?" She points in their direction.

"They're not dipwads. They're my friends."

"Your friends? The same ones who threw popcorn at us on the bus? Those animals are not your friends."

"Josh didn't do that. He never does anything bad."

"Oh yeah?" Lenora looks over my shoulder at the guys. "Does he ever stick up for you?"

I don't answer her. I just shake my knee and turn my head, so I can see the guys out of the corner of my eye.

"Because a true friend would stick up for you." She pops a grape into her mouth. "Just sayin'."

"Whatever." I unwrap my sandwich. "You don't understand."

"Obviously. Why do you want to be friends with them?"

I push my sandwich away. I'm not hungry. "Why do you want to be friends with the Barbie Dolls?"

"I *don't* want to be friends with them. I want to be friends with *you*."

"Why?" I watch Josh and Snake as they laugh at something Frankie said.

Lenora gets up and tosses her lunch wrappers in the trash. "Stop your pity party. Geez. You're a good guy. And if they can't see that on their own, no amount of magic will change it."

THURSDAY–STILL AT THE MUSEUM

After lunch is the part of the tour that everyone's been looking forward to—the "scary" hieroglyphics tunnel. The students who went to the museum last year couldn't stop talking about it. It's dimly lit and supposed to make you think you're in an ancient pyramid or something.

I try to get excited, but mostly I'm thinking about what Lenora said. Maybe she's right. But I can't help thinking that if the guys knew I wasn't lying, everything would be okay again. Like it used to be.

We all head into the tunnel, and honestly, it's not as spooky as everyone wants to pretend. The colors change from green to red to yellow, and the light is a little low, but you can still totally see everything. Some of the kids start shrieking in fake squeals like they're afraid when we all know they totally aren't. Lenora sticks pretty close to me and rolls her eyes every time someone shrieks.

I'm toward the middle of the tunnel when someone yanks my backpack off my left shoulder. I whip around and see Frankie toss it back to Alex.

"Give it back!" I yell.

Alex unzips it and pulls out the wooden box. "Snake, catch!"

He tosses it to Snake, who opens the box and lifts out the pouch. "Oooh, the magic is overpowering me!"

I push back against the crowd moving through the tunnel. "Snake, don't. Give it back."

Snake drops the box and holds the pouch up, waving it at me like I'm a dog and it's a chew toy. "You want it?" he teases.

I shove a bunch of kids out of the way, and someone yells, "Get off my feet!" and pushes back. When I get within reach of Snake, he tosses the pouch high over my head to Alex.

"Here, boy. Come and get it," Alex taunts. I jostle toward him, but he throws the pouch to Frankie. Instead, it hits Nicole on the back of the head.

"Ow. What was that?" she cries.

I can't see where the pouch landed, but it must be on the ground by Nicole. Frankie's much closer to her than me, so I dive for it. So does Frankie. We crash into Nicole and all fall to the ground. I land on top of Nicole, who's on top of Frankie. It's a Nicole sandwich.

"Get off me!" she shouts. "Mr. Widelot!"

I spy the pouch on the ground next to Nicole's shoulder. I grab it and roll off her, crawling on hands and knees through the crowd until I can stand up. I look around. I'm right by the exit. No sign of Widelot, thankfully, because I'm sure any second Nicole will rat me out for tackling her.

I scoot through the tunnel's exit and slump down against the wall of the gallery, facing the creepy mummy from this morning. Kids pour out of the tunnel and wander around the gallery. No one seems to notice me sitting on the ground. At least no teachers have screamed at me yet to get up. I have no clue where my backpack or the wooden box are, but at least I have the magic pouch. I should use it to make that disgusting mummy and scare the pants off Snake.

No! No, I shouldn't!

What am I thinking?

I'm *not* thinking.

I have the pouch.

In my hand.

Oh no.

The pouch starts to bulge and wiggle. *Please be a three-headed tree frog.*

I drop the pouch—fast. And it's a good thing I do because it's not a frog. It's a fleshy, rotting mummy poking out of the opening.

I stare in disbelief as the miniature mummy hobbles away, its leg bones barely covered in some pinkish, brownish stuff that probably used to be flesh.

I should pick it up. I know I should. But it's so . . . gross.

The mummy heads directly into the group of kids still wandering through the tunnel. Their now perfectly real screams defy all laws of physics. They run out of the tunnel, ranting to the disbelief of the teachers.

"Did you see that? Disgusting!"

"What was that?"

"Ewwwwwww!"

"There was a tiny mummy in the tunnel!"

I pinch the magic pouch by its drawstring and zip back through the tunnel exit. It's nearly empty now and much easier to see. I spot the mummy immediately, pitching from side to side and bumping into the walls.

I race in and slide down on the ground, holding the

pouch open a foot from the wobbling, fleshy mess. "Here, mummy, mummy." *Please, please, please go in.*

But instead, it lobs to the right, hugging the wall, and heads for the entrance. Which Mr. Widelot is about to walk through.

Oh great.

I leap to my feet, stepping toward my teacher. Thankfully the light is dimmer against the wall where the mummy is currently stumbling. Hopefully Mr. Widelot won't notice.

"Oh, hey, Mr. Widelot. Um, what's up?" I stand as tall as possible, trying to keep his eyes away from the ground.

Mr. Widelot crosses his arms. "Mr. Hopper. Was that you scaring everyone?"

"Um . . ." I reflexively side-eye the mummy to our right.

Mr. Widelot takes several steps forward and stops, looking down his nose at me. The staggering mummy is behind him now, but Mr. Widelot has managed to step on some of the unraveled bandages. As the mummy continues to zombie-walk toward the entrance, it loses more and more coverage. I can barely stand to look at its rotting behind.

"What are you holding?" Mr. Widelot points to the

pouch I'm holding by its drawstrings. "Does that belong to the museum?"

"No. It's nothing."

"Let me see, please." He leans in closer and swipes it from my clutch.

Oh, great. Knowing him, he'll confiscate it and use it to store caramels or something.

"It's my . . . lunch bag. I got it from my gram." Not a total lie.

Mr. Widelot holds it up to get a better look in the dim light. "Hmm."

"Can I have it back? Please?" I have one eye on my teacher, one eye on my pouch, and one eye on the stumbling mummy, which is one too many eyes, I know, but anyway.

"What were you doing in here alone?" Mr. Widelot thrusts the pouch back at me, and I let out a huge breath.

"Someone took my backpack. I came in to look for it."

The mummy is right behind Mr. Widelot now, loping this way and that. I watch, trying not to be obvious about it.

Mr. Widelot narrows his gaze. "You didn't cause the screaming?"

"Ah . . ."

The mummy starts ambling back toward us. In about

three seconds, a nearly naked, rotting, six-inch Egyptian corpse is going to bump straight into the back of Mr. Widelot's legs.

"I'm waiting." He stands, hands on hips, legs apart.

Since he already hates me and thinks I'm weird, I do the only thing I can think of. I dive-crawl through his legs, pouch outstretched, aimed at the mummy.

"What on earth?" Mr. Widelot exclaims as I push against his parted knees.

I wrinkle my nostrils and hold the pouch open in the path of the mummy, right behind Mr. Widelot's legs. With me tangled up in his legs he can't turn around. I just pray my body is blocking his view.

"What are you doing? Get up this minute."

The nasty mummy practically falls on the pouch's opening. I try to scoop him in without touching any of his putrefied carcass. *Blech.*

Mr. Widelot finally gets untangled and tugs at my shirt collar, hoisting me up. "Have you lost your mind?"

As he does, I press the pouch to my chest. And—sigh of relief—it's empty. Marvelously, spectacularly empty. The naked mummy, minus his unraveled wrappings, has gone back to the Other Realm it came from.

"I thought I saw my backpack," I say.

Mr. Widelot shakes his head. "Honestly, Westin, I just

don't understand you. Find your stuff. We're leaving now. Back on the bus in the same seats." He turns and walks out the exit.

I let out a breath. That was way, *way* too close. Skimming the floor for my backpack, I spot it and the wooden box tucked in a corner. I slip the magic pouch back inside the box and put the box in my backpack before I manage to conjure anything else creepy and disgusting. I'm sure the museum folks are going to be scratching their heads over the tiny mummy wrappings they find on the tunnel floor.

Just in time, I head to the bus, so *so* thankful I'm not bringing a dead pharaoh home with me. A growing T. rex is one thing. But a zombie? At that point, I'd just shut my bedroom door and walk away.

THURSDAY—ON THE BUS

I get on the bus and throw myself down on the seat next to Lenora. My face is on fire, and I'm breathing hard. The bus is buzzing with chatter about whatever the creepy thing was, wrapped in rotting bandages and limping through the end of the tunnel.

"You look like your head's going to pop off," Lenora says. "What the heck happened back there?"

"A tiny mummy happened."

She flinches away from me, eyes wide. "You didn't. That's what everyone is talking about? From the pouch? Is it in your pack?"

"Yeah."

"Gross! You brought the mummy on the bus?" she screeches.

"No, *shh!*" I clasp my hand over her mouth and look around. "The *magic pouch* is in my pack. I got it back from the guys. But then I sort of accidentally conjured the mummy dude. And accidentally let it out of the pouch. And accidentally scared everyone. I got it to go back in right before it accidentally bumped into Widelot. It's gone now."

Lenora's mouth drops.

"I've had a very eventful museum visit."

"I'll say." She crosses her arms. "You shouldn't have brought the pouch. You've already broken the one and only code you made for yourself, and it's been like two seconds."

I let out a puff of air. "I decided to bring it before I made the code. Anyway, I just wanted to show my friends. Here's what I don't get, though. Why would I be able to make the mummy but not make the three headed-tree frog?"

"What three-headed tree frog?"

"Doesn't matter." I wave my hand. "Why some things and not others?"

Lenora shrugs, and I think about the card that came with the pouch. I've practically memorized it by now.

Customized enchantmen, conjured by the eye . . . and just then, I have one of those genius thoughts that rarely strike.

"Wait a minute. Wait, wait, wait." I sit up. "So far, everything that's come out of that pouch has been something I've *seen*."

"So?" Lenora says.

"So I can't conjure it if I haven't seen it."

"I don't get what you mean."

"It's like it says on that card—*enchantment, conjured by the eye*. The turtle painting, my rubber T. rex, my army men . . . they were all things I *saw*. Not things I imagined. When I hold the pouch and imagine the T. rex going back, that's not something I could ever see with my eyes. So I can't conjure it." I bounce in my seat because I know I'm right.

"Hold on." Lenora puts up a palm. "What about Thor? And that owl? Those came out of your brain, dude."

"Nope! They came from movies I *saw*. I was thinking about those movies when it happened."

"Okay, say your theory is right." Lenora shrugs. "That's not exactly good news. If you can only conjure what you see, how are you ever going to get rid of your prehistoric houseguest?"

"That is the ten-million-dollar question," I say.

Lenora and I sit in silence for a while, thinking. The bus

motor whirs underneath me and makes my skin vibrate. Finally, Lenora speaks. "Maybe you could try wrangling the pouch onto Tiny T's head. Maybe you could force him in."

I motion to my skinny arms. "With these muscles? Even if I pumped weights in the smelly school gym, it's hopeless. I'd never stand a chance against a T. rex," I say. "Those teeth? His claws? He already nailed me once, and I'm probably going to die from dinosaur-itis." I brush my hand over the brownish scab on my leg. "We're doomed."

She pushes me in the side. "You'll figure it out. I believe in you."

"That makes one of us."

"Hey, don't be so hard on yourself. You found a magic pouch in your grandma's basement. So that means . . ." Lenora splays her hands like I'm supposed to fill in the blank.

". . . that means I was poking around where Pops doesn't allow?" I ask.

"No, it means you're *curious*. That's a very positive quality."

I shrug. "If you say so."

"Think about it. You could have made something simple and boring—like a wad of cash or a new computer. But you made a T. rex!"

I laugh. "Yeah, because Brain was on vacation."

"Your brain's *adventurous*!" she insists. "You made an army to trap the dinosaur. And you figured out how to get him into your closet. And you thought to go to your grandma's to find answers. And you figured out how to open the wooden box. And—"

"Okay, okay." I shake my head.

"Creative thinker!" She laughs.

"Flaky thinker," I correct.

"High energy, that's all." She elbows me. "Which means you are never boring! And you offered to make something for me. So you're a good friend."

I sigh. "Thanks for the pep talk. But none of those things will get Tiny T out of my room."

Lenora sinks down and swings her feet up to rest on the seat in front of her. "Maybe we can trap him, like in a cage. Dad has one he uses to get raccoons that steal the eggs. Then we can let him go somewhere far away."

"He's *growing*. If he'd stay small forever, I could do that. In fact, I would totally keep him. But who knows how big he'll get. As tall as a skyscraper. He might eat San Francisco. Then . . . the world!"

"Yeah, I guess. Can you imagine?" She bursts out laughing.

I can't help it. I do too.

"Oh, noooo. Help! A giant T. rex is devouring my building! I paid a lot for this condo!" Lenora screeches in a pretend grown-up voice.

"Six o'clock news reporting live. Crowds cheer as an enormous reptile has bitten off the top of the new Salesforce Tower. Authorities are warning people to stay away from skyscrapers." I laugh.

"And try not to look like salami!" Lenora adds, holding her sides. "Thank goodness for Thor, really. Otherwise your whole house would be torn apart, not just your room."

I snort. "Thor. 'Stand aside while I show off my mythical awesomeness!'"

She laughs. "You jealous of a foot-high guy in fur?"

"Not *jealous*." I snort again.

Lenora flicks her red hair behind her shoulder. "I can't help the effect I have on him. Mom was a model."

Poor Lenora. She must miss her mom so much. I wonder if any of the things she says about her are true. I kind of want to ask, but then again, I don't want her to think I don't believe her. I know how it feels when your friends think you're lying.

"Thor's helpful, no doubt," I say. "But he'd be a lot more helpful if he could tell me how to send Tiny T back."

"Do you think . . ." Lenora pauses. "Can the pouch make real people, not just imaginary ones like Thor?"

I tap my thumbs on my knees. "I don't know. The mummy I made today was a real person once, but he still came back dead. And gross."

"Hmmm." Lenora nods and chews on her bottom lip. "Why?"

She doesn't answer. Just stares out the window.

"If you want me to make some movie star you have a crush on, you can forget about it."

That doesn't make her laugh. She shrugs. "I was just wondering."

We ride in silence again. I drum my fingers on the back of the seat in front of me.

"So . . . um. West?" she finally says.

"Yeah?'

"I was thinking. . . . Can you stop drumming for a second?" Lenora twists her mouth.

"I thought you didn't mind it?"

"I know but . . ." Lenora chews on the end of her hoodie tie.

I stop. "Okay."

"I was wondering. And, um, I'm . . ."

I pick up a blue bottle cap from the floor and toss it with my right hand and catch it with my left, back and forth.

"... pretty sure ..." she continues. "Will you stop with that cap?"

"Oh, sorry." I keep the cap in my hand.

"As I was saying. I was thinking about the magic, and I—"

I start to flick the edge of the cap with my thumbnail. *Flick. Flick. Flick.*

"Seriously," she says. "Can you just focus for a second?"

"But you said it didn't both—"

"I'm trying to talk!"

Just then the bus makes a sharp right turn into the school, and Lenora leans into me. I almost fall off the seat into the aisle. She scoots back toward the window as the bus comes to a stop. The driver opens the door with a loud *whoosh.*

"Anyway. Um ... West?"

"Yeah?"

"I know we've only been friends for like. . . a few days. But . . ."

Warning, warning! Gobbledy-gook alert! She's going to say how much our friendship means or . . . oh, crud, something even worse. I tense and suck my top lip in, closing my eyes against the uncomfortable glob of ickiness.

". . . I decided what I want from the magic pouch. And . . . it's kind of, well . . ." Her voice trails in a whisper.

I exhale. No gobbledy-gook! She wants me to make her something.

I turn and smile. "What is it? Money? Jewels?"

Lenora looks like she might cry. Softly, barely audible over the drone of the kids filing off the bus, she replies. "My mom."

THURSDAY, STILL ON THE BUS—SPEECHLESS FOR ONCE

The skin on the back of my neck prickles. I can't do that. There's no way. I'm sure if my mom died, I'd wish for the same thing. But she can't be serious.

Lenora looks at me like a hopeful puppy desperate for a treat.

"Lenora, I can't." I stand up and wait for the kids in front to get off the bus.

"Why not?" She slumps.

"Who knows what could happen? That's got to be against the code," I whisper as kids file past.

"You just invented that code. And, technically, there's only one rule, which you immediately broke when it was convenient for you."

"Yeah. But, this type of thing is exactly *why* we need a code."

Snake passes by and hip checks me, but I ignore him.

"What about a friendship code?" Lenora asks, her voice getting louder and higher pitched. "I just want to talk to her one time. One conversation." She stands, her eyes wide and pleading.

"I don't know, Lenora . . ."

"Please, pretty please. I'll be your loyal and true best friend forever. Always by your side, through thick and thin." Her hands are clasped in front of her chin, begging. "I would never throw popcorn at the back of your head."

What she's saying is tempting. It would be super nice to have a loyal friend I could always count on. And Lenora is mega fun. Truthfully, she's way nicer to me than Josh and Snake are. Maybe I should do this for her. It certainly couldn't be worse than a T. rex. Maybe it would feel good to do something nice for someone and make that person happy instead of, say, giving someone a black eye and making that person hate you.

I look at Lenora as she bats her eyelashes, and I imagine what it would be like to see her mom crawl out of my pouch. She'd be six inches high. That would be weird. No one wants a six-inch-high mom. What if she came out a zombie, like the pharaoh? She did die, after all.

Shivers run down my spine. Even act-before-you-think Westin knows this is a bad idea.

"But . . . remember?" I say, searching for a reason to say no. "I can only conjure things I've seen. I've never seen your mom." The bus is now completely empty.

"You could look at photos. I could tell you about her."

"I can't . . ." I look down and kick at the seat leg.

"You mean, you won't." Lenora picks up her backpack and slings it over her shoulder, whacking me in the chest with it.

"Lenora." I tug at a tear in the back of the vinyl seat cover. "I get it. I do. I'd give anything to see Uncle Marty again. And this is your mom. I can't even imagine what it must be like. But . . . the thing is, you never even knew her. Right? How could you tell me what she was like?"

Lenora puts a hand to her chest, like I kicked her there. Almost too quietly, she says, "That's possibly the worst thing anyone has ever said to me."

Without another word, she pushes past me, stomping down the aisle.

"Lenora! Come on. I'm sorry. I didn't mean it like that."

She doesn't look back. I run after her.

"Lenora, wait!"

"You're supposed to help friends!" she yells behind her. "Maybe that's why you don't have any anymore."

Ouch.

She keeps moving, marching toward a blue bike locked with a long chain in the school bike barn.

"I just meant . . . think about it," I plead. "She'd come out six inches tall, like Thor and the mummy did. What are you going to do with a tiny mom? Lenora, I can't do that."

She stops. "I don't care if she's tiny!"

"Are you listening to yourself? Haven't you ever seen a horror movie? It never works out the way you want."

She huffs.

"And I haven't figured out how to send things back yet. You'd just, what? Hide your six-inch mom in my closet with a T. rex?"

The chain clinks against the stem of the bike as Lenora unravels and plops it into her front basket. She's going to yell at me. Start screaming any minute. I just know it.

But instead, Lenora does something worse. She starts to cry. Not a loud wailing cry. More of a wet sniffle. Sometimes that's harder to watch.

"I'm super sorry," I say.

"You don't understand." Lenora cries softly. "Your mom is still alive. I don't remember mine. Not at all." Her crying starts to get bigger, the tears dripping off her cheeks. "You're right. I have no idea what she was like. She wasn't a ballet dancer or a yoga teacher or an artist or a model. I don't know anything about her because no one ever talks about her."

That makes sense, but it makes me feel a thousand times worse too.

"Maybe you could ask your dad? Like I asked Gram about Uncle Marty. Your dad's so nice. And he cares a lot about you. I mean, I wish my dad was like that."

Lenora wipes her eyes with her sleeve. "I've tried. He always changes the subject."

"Maybe Grannie then? What if you ask her?"

"Grannie? The one who . . ." Lenora sucks in a sob. ". . . *cooked* . . . the only other thing I loved?" Her shoulders start to shake. "I want to meet her. Just once. Even if she's tiny. I could hold onto that forever."

I stand in front of her, not knowing what to do with my hands. It seems like I should hug her or something, but that's too weird. "Um. I'm really sorry you didn't know your mom."

Lenora takes in another sobby breath and looks up

at me, so hopeful. I start to fiddle with the chain and lock, lifting it out of her bike basket.

"I know how much you want this. But I think it's a bad idea," I whisper, still fumbling with the chain. To no one's surprise, it slips through my fingers and lands on her toes.

"Ow! West, what's wrong with you?" Her face is red and moist, and she wipes at it with the back of her hand. "Can't you just stop for once?"

"Sorry. Vacation Brain . . ."

"Stop blaming your brain," Lenora snaps. "Your brain is you."

Her words are a swift kick in the groin. Vacation Brain isn't me. I thought she understood.

"You have this epic thing, West. You could do so much with that magic. Anything! All you do is destroy half your room with ridiculous creatures." She throws her hands in the air.

I take a step back. "But not this, Lenora. Can't you see? That's why we should have a code—"

"Sure! Great! Make your stupid code. Then you can break it right away for your *friends*. You know, the ones who clearly hate you. I hope that works out for you." She swings her leg over the bike and pushes me out of her way with her shoulder.

I stand there, mouth open, holding back tears. It feels like Thor whacked me in the stomach. This has got to be a record. Friend made and lost in forty-eight hours. Triple dang it.

THURSDAY NIGHT

Mom is furious. Rotor blades are whirring so fast, the gale force nearly knocks me over.

"How do you *miss* carpool?"

I toss my backpack on the floor of the car and slam the door. Five minutes late. I only took five minutes to talk to Lenora, and Nicole seized the opportunity to convince her mom to leave without me. Probably made up some story about how I tackled her at the museum and got detention.

Well, I guess that's sort of true. I *did* tackle her at the museum. And I *did* get detention—just not for this.

"I'm so sorry, Mom."

"You absolutely cannot, under any circumstances,

miss carpool tomorrow. I have an extremely important meeting in the city that I can't leave. Do you understand? I'm giving a presentation at a conference, and I won't even have my phone on in case you call."

I nod.

"All you have to do is get to the car line and wait for your ride. What were you doing anyway? You didn't get detention, did you? Did you get in trouble on the field trip?"

Yes, and yes. Man, I'm like an open book. But neither of those truths are why I was late.

"Um, I made a new friend. And, well . . . her mom died. And she was super sad about it and needed someone to talk to, so I stayed late to listen."

This partly true lie is brought to you for two reasons:

Mom is a total softie when it comes to helping people with their problems.

She'll be ecstatic I made a new friend.

"You have a new friend?"

Bingo.

I nod.

"Well . . . I'm proud of you for being a good friend. But I can't be coming to work late and leaving early, buddy. Especially tomorrow."

I nod. Here's hoping tomorrow won't involve me bringing a mummy—or anything else—to life.

When we arrive home, I go directly to the fridge and pull out a chunk of salami for T, plus a slice of leftover pizza for myself. I'm starving after a long day of alarms, mummies, and disappointing my new friend. There's about an inch less of salami today, so I'm betting Thor got some to feed T. At least he didn't leave a mess this time.

"Hmm, where's Fiddles?" Mom asks.

"Dunno." I slam the fridge door and head down the hall to my room, munching the cold pizza.

"How's your room coming along?" Mom yells after me. "Can we put Cappuccino back in there yet? Do you need any help? I have storage bins if you want them."

"Nope!" I yell back, opening my bedroom door. As I do, I think about what Mom said about Fiddles. She always comes to the kitchen when we get home. But today she didn't. She's nowhere in sight.

My heart jumps to my throat. What if she got in my room when Thor came out to feed Tiny T?

Oh no. Please no.

I'm afraid to open my eyes. When I do, I'm not ready for what I see.

Fiddles is on the carpet by the bookshelf. Her collar is off, and she's not moving. And holy, holy crud! Tiny T is loose in my room.

Oh no, he killed her. He did it.

My hand flies to my mouth. "Oh, Fiddles."

Her feline head pops up, and I jump. She's not dead! She was . . . sleeping? With a T. rex running around? A T. rex who is currently *charging right toward her*!

"Fiddles, run!" I yell.

Thor, trying to capture T, has climbed on his back and is swinging his hammer in the air. And Tiny T is not so tiny. He's as big as a very large raccoon now.

Fiddles has got to be the most dimwitted cat in the entire world. She doesn't move. She's completely oblivious, not even remotely concerned that she's about to get demolished by a reptile with fangs. Instead, she starts preening herself.

I charge toward her. "Fiddles, run!" I wave my arms.

"What's going on in there, hon?" Mom yells from the kitchen.

I grab Fiddles and swoop her up. Thor is still on T's back, coming right at my shins, and I have nowhere to go.

"Faster, you beast!" Thor yells.

Faster?

Just before careening into me, T veers left and circles toward the closet, narrowly missing chewing off my legs. That's when I notice that Thor is holding onto a pink collar around T's neck—Fiddles's collar.

"Are you *riding* him?" I ask in disbelief.

The army men are lined up by the closet, jumping up and down. Cheering Thor on.

"We have reached a truce, your mighty dragon and I. He is actually quite an agreeable fellow!"

Fiddles tries to wiggle out of my arms, but I clasp tight. "You reached a *truce*?" Thor and the T. rex whip by me again, and I flinch. "He let you put Fiddles's collar on and ride him?"

Thor pulls not-so-Tiny T to a stop. T bends down, and Thor hops off his back. T is panting as he faces Fiddles and me, saliva dripping from the sharp tips of his teeth, almost like he's . . . drooling. For dinner.

The hairs rise on my neck, and I step back toward the door. Any minute now he's gonna charge us. Suddenly Fiddles wriggles free and leaps at T and Thor.

"No!" I reach for my cat as she rolls onto her back, completely unaware that she's about to be dino-dinner. "Thor, don't let him eat her!"

In a flash, Tiny T lowers his angular jaws in her direction. I thrust my hands out, just as T lunges at Fiddles's belly.

"Fiddles!" I cry.

But I can't get to her in time. Tiny T is on her and . . . wait. *He's rubbing his face in her fur*?

Fiddles swats playfully at Tiny T's head, like she does to me when I tickle her. T just rubs some more, getting the fur on her belly wet with his drool. Fiddles bats at him a few more times, then bounds to her feet and leaps onto the bookshelf.

"What the heck?" I let out the giant breath I was holding. "I thought he was going to eat her."

Thor laughs. "Nonsense. He prefers that flat red meat you serve. Salami."

Tiny T cocks his head, like a dog hearing the word *walk*. Spying the food in my clenched fist, he ambles over to me and sits, arms hanging, tongue wagging—like he's begging.

This is unbelievable. My dinosaur and my cat are now friends. My small Norse god likes to ride said dinosaur. And my headless zombie army likes to cheer them on.

My life is insane. (And also, awesome.)

I kneel and slowly extend my hand, offering T the salami. This might possibly be the stupidest thing I've ever done. In thirty seconds, I could be missing my right hand. I should throw the food on the floor, of course, but I guess Vacation Brain is at a show in Vegas.

T sniffs and takes a step forward, then another, until he is inches from my extended hand. He bends slightly and gently tugs at the meat with his mouth, his eyes on mine the whole time.

I don't move my hand, and once he's done eating, he does the most unexpected thing. He rubs the side of his face in my palm, just like Fiddles does when she wants her chin rubbed.

My heart thumps madly. I just *hand-fed* a T. rex.

I reach forward and slowly stroke Tiny T's chin. He immediately falls to his back on the ground, and I jump. The green army men rush to him and climb over each other to scratch his chin and belly. The T. rex moans, low and growly.

"He enjoys a good scratching," says Thor. "The men attend to him when he reclines. Their hard-skinned surface works well on dragonian hide."

"How did you get him like this?" Kneeling, I scoot close to T and the men. This is crazy. He's docile. I don't care how big he gets. I'm totally keeping him.

"We tamed him. We have been sharing the dungeon for days. These things happen." Thor climbs onto T's tail and is lifted high into the air. Hanging on with one hand, Thor waves his mallet, as if he's riding a bull.

After a moment, T curls his tail and deposits Thor onto his belly. "I am pleased I did not have to kill you, wingless dragon," Thor says, rubbing him hard.

I lean forward and, keeping my eyes on T's mouth, slowly extend my hand to pat his belly. His skin is cold and dimply like a basketball.

There's a knock on my door. "Buddy, dinner in fifteen minutes."

At the sound of Mom's voice, T jumps to his feet, throwing Thor off his belly and startling the army men. I leap back and pick up my plastic trash bin to shield myself if he attacks.

Thor raises his hands. "Calm yourself, mighty one. It is only the ogre's mother."

T bends toward Thor with his mouth slightly open, and for a second, I think the mini god is toast. But instead, T licks Thor's face, and the army men jump with excitement.

Thor wipes his face with the back of his hand. "They think it's amusing because they know it displeases me. My lady should not delight in the smell of dragon spit on my face."

I'm pretty sure Lenora won't care what Thor smells like, but I *so* wish she were here to see this. Maybe then she'd forget she's mad at me.

I grab my phone and check that it's fully charged. I'm not taking lame blurry photos this time. This time, Lenora and the guys are going to get their minds blown.

"Let's give the nonbelievers something good to see!" I announce.

In a few minutes, I have an obstacle course set up on the floor of my room. I use old train tracks, blocks, and books. The course has curves and jumps; it winds around the room, over the bed, and through the closet.

Thor mounts T, and when I say "Go!" he races though the course with Fiddles casually looking on. I clock how fast they go, recording the whole thing on my phone, and with each run, they beat their previous time.

"Two minutes and twelve seconds! A dinosaur world record!" I high-five Thor's small hand—after teaching him what it means—and he slides down T's back to the floor.

"There's no way Josh and Snake won't believe me now," I say. "Once Lenora and the guys see this, everything will be normal, and we can be friends again."

"Ogre. You are proving to be among the more pleasant monsters I have encountered. At the very least, I am not of frequent mind to slay you. However, if this is the recourse to win friends, then these ogres seem but foes in disguise." Thor rubs his little chin. "This is of great concern."

"You're pretty cool too, Thor. But you don't have to worry about me."

"Is my lady among these ogres' enemies?" He raises his mallet. "I shall have to bring them to their knees if they harm her."

Guess it's not me he's worried about, after all.

"They're not enemies. And you don't have to worry about Lenora. She can take care of herself."

"Shall we go one more course with the great dragon, then?" Thor begins to mount T.

Before I can answer, T falls to his front and then flops to his side, panting. I kneel beside him, and Thor climbs onto his belly.

"What's wrong with him?" I place my hand on T's chest. His breathing is fast, and I can feel his T. rex heart beating wildly. Not in a rhythm—more like a ball bouncing off walls.

"He spent the morning on his side, breathing like this," Thor replies. "After I fed him, he rose. However, I fear your flat, red meat may not be enough to sustain him. Alas, Mjolnir struck to the cranium ofttimes brings many a beast to its demise."

My own heart beats faster. Poor guy. Thwacked on the head too many times *and* he needs more food. I grab my blue fleece blanket with the white baseballs and one of my sweatshirts and make a little T. rex bed for him on the floor.

"You guys don't have to sleep in the closet anymore. Now that I know he won't kill me." I pat T's head. "It's okay, buddy. I'm going to bring you dinner. I bet you'd love cat food. Right, Fiddles? Hang in there, T."

Thor and the men curl up next to T.

"Or . . . maybe you want to go home now?" I'd die to keep T. Especially since he's turning out to be the coolest T. rex in the world. But he's growing and needs real T. rex food—whatever that is. I sort of don't want to know.

I pull the wooden box from my backpack, carry it over to Tiny T, and drop the magic pouch down by his side. Just in case he decides to go back in—somehow. Even though he's now about fifteen thousand times bigger than the pouch.

But he doesn't move.

"I have to go eat my dinner. Then I'll bring food."

"We shall stay with your dragon, ogre," Thor says.

"Thanks."

Fiddles jumps off the bookshelf and swaggers over to where T lays on the blanket. She curls herself up into the nook of his belly and starts to lick her tail. It's so cute. I wish I could show someone. That's the worst part of having friends who are mad at you. I have this totally awesome thing, and no one to share it with.

FRIDAY

When I wake in the morning, T is still curled up on his little blanket on the floor at the foot of my bed. Thor is huddled by his belly, still sleeping, while the army men stand guard.

Fiddles scratches at my door to be let out, so I put her collar back on and open the door. Then I slip the magic pouch back into the wooden box and into my backpack. Today I'm going to prove to Josh and Snake that I'm not making this stuff up.

I tiptoe out and, when Mom isn't looking, stock up on more cat food, leftover meatloaf, and water for T's bowl. Thor and Tiny T don't wake before I leave. I guess the big night of obstacle course racing wore everyone out.

At school, Lenora hops out of her dad's truck, and I run over to her. She's wearing a Giants cap, and it stops me in my tracks. *The Giants?*

She pushes past me without even looking.

"Lenora?"

She keeps walking. "Hey, Alicia! Wait up!"

"Come on, Lenora!" I say.

She picks up her pace.

I chase after her until I'm close enough to whisper, "The T. rex is tamed. Thor can ride him now. I have video."

"Don't care." Lenora catches up to Alicia and says something into her ear, making Alicia laugh.

I stand there and watch them run off as the first bell rings. Lenora's so mad she's done the unthinkable—gone over to the Barbie side.

When I run into class, Mr. Widelot stares me down. I can't even begin to decipher today's shirt.

SHUT YOUR
π
HOLE

I can feel his eyes on me as I zip to my seat. It's creepy that he still hasn't said a thing about me not showing up for detention four days straight.

Mr. Widelot claps his hands. "Okay, mathletes, today is Friday. You all know what that means." He glances at his desk and the large basket filled with colorfully wrapped candy that will never enter my mouth.

"Candy Friday!" everyone yells.

"That's right, Candy Friday. Are we ready to tally the points?"

"Yeah!"

I take a deep breath. This will go one of two ways, and both are usually disappointing.

"Let's see. On Monday, things went well until a student got detention. So that's six out of seven points. Not bad."

The class claps. I don't. He mentioned the detention.

"Then Tuesday," Mr. Widelot continues. "As a class, you earned a full seven points. Congratulations. But that student never showed up for Monday's detention, so that's minus a point."

So that's how he's going to play this. This whole time he was just waiting to see if I'd show.

"Can anyone tell me how many points we have now?" Mr. Widelot asks.

Nicole shoots up her hand. "Twelve out of thirty-five total, with a minimum of twenty-five necessary for candy."

"Thank you, Nicole. So, Wednesday. Wednesday was an extremely unfortunate day, and we don't need to dwell on the reason why. Needless to say, a poor choice was made in tech class, which resulted in only three points that day. Nicole?"

I sigh as we enter extremely familiar territory where candy does not appear.

Nicole turns to me and twists her mouth. "A total of fifteen points."

"And unfortunately, the student who received detention did not show up on Tuesday either," Mr. Widelot says. "Minus another point."

I slump a little lower in my desk.

"Fourteen points," Nicole says glumly.

"Thursday," Mr. Widelot says. "The class behaved . . . interestingly. The alarm set off by Mr. Hopper cost a point. And the screaming fit at the end—I'm not sure what that was, so we'll just leave it alone. I'll give you six for the day."

The class moans. But let's be real—that could've gone much worse.

"Unfortunately, the student missed detention again on Wednesday. So even though the class had six points for yesterday, I am afraid you can only keep five."

I don't know why he keeps saying *student*. Everyone knows it's me. If the stares of my classmates could burn my clothes to a crisp, I'd already be naked.

"Nineteen total," Nicole says.

"So how many do we need today?" Mr. Widelot asks. "Westin?"

"Six." I groan. "Six points to get to twenty-five."

"And did the student come to detention yesterday?"

My shoulders slump. "No."

The class grumbles.

"So six is the maximum we can possibly get," Nicole calculates. "Since we already lost a point because—*ahem*—someone *forgot* to go to detention. *Again.*"

Mr. Widelot nods. "That is correct. Everyone needs to be on their best behavior for class today. There is no room for error. Shall we begin?"

Nicole sits up straight and readies her pencil. Mr. Widelot starts droning on about adding one-half to three-fourths.

I doodle in my notebook: a picture of Thor sitting on my shoulder while we walk T on a leash through the park. As I draw, I think. Lenora has no right to be mad at me. I met her five days ago, and she expects me to resurrect her mom? When she knows it might not even work? That's a lot to ask of a brand-new friend.

Plus, that stuff she said. First, she points out all my positive qualities, and then she takes it all away. *Your brain is you.* That wasn't nice. Maybe she wasn't a real friend. Maybe she just liked me for my magic.

I look at the back of Snake's head three seats away. While Mr. Widelot faces the board, Snake flicks a folded paper football through Josh's finger upright two rows over. It misses by a mile, and the football lands on the floor by my foot.

I lean down to grab it, but Mr. Widelot turns around at that exact moment. His gaze zooms straight to the paper triangle in my hand. "Mr. Hopper? A paper football?"

I glance at Josh. His eyes are pleading for me to keep quiet, and I'm torn. Do I tell the truth, that it belongs to Snake? Telling on them will only make my life ten thousand times worse. Not telling on them could make things better. Show that I'm one of them.

"It's not mine," I say. "I was just picking it up."

Mr. Widelot takes a step toward my desk. "Whose is it, then?"

No one moves. The plan for a late-morning sugar high just went south.

"Well?"

Me? Why me? Why won't someone else just yell out, "Snake did it!" and save me?

I hunch both shoulders.

Mr. Widelot exhales loudly. "Westin, I'm at a loss. I can't have the constant distractions. I think you should go to the office for the rest of class."

"But it wasn't me!"

I look over at Josh, wishing he'd defend me. But he and Snake just slump down in their seats.

Mr. Widelot nods to the door. "Come on. And no candy this week. Sorry, kids."

The class moans. "Hyper Hopper blows it *again*," Nicole mutters.

I grab my backpack and try to make eye contact with Josh as I leave. He looks away, and I slam the door behind me. I'm starting to wonder if the code is a bad idea—a house-smashing robot sounds pretty good right now.

In the office, I crash down on the hard wooden bench at the Wall of Shame. This bench should have a metal plate with my name on it:

In honor of Westin Scott Hopper. Because his butt warms it at least once a week.

I swing my legs back and forth, the rubber from my sneakers squeaking against the floor as they brush past and come to a stop. *Screech. Thwamp. Screech. Thwamp.*

Mrs. Sandbeam, the office assistant, raises an eyebrow. "Stop squeaking, West. You're giving me a headache."

I pull out my sketchpad and flip through the pages until I come to a blank one. Some of the pages are tearing away from the metal rings because I don't always close the sketchbook when I'm done. The fire monster that I finished at Gram's slips off and flutters to the floor, landing at Mrs. Sandbeam's feet. She picks it up.

"Where did you get this?" she asks.

I stand up and take the drawing from her. "No place." I put it on top of my sketchbook.

"I love his giant eyes. And these flames. It's really good. Did you draw that?"

I shrug.

"You're very talented." Mrs. Sandbeam says it like she's surprised.

Just then the class bell rings, signaling first recess. It's Friday, which can only mean one thing: It's Friendship Group time.

Time to face Lenora.

FRIDAY–FIRST RECESS

"What does it mean to be a friend, Steve?" Ms. Molly stands by the whiteboard in the counseling room, ready to write down the incredible words of middle-school wisdom we blurt out.

Lenora sits next to me, not by choice, but because it was the only open seat when she came in. She won't look at me, and she's biting her upper lip so hard I'm worried she might leave permanent teeth marks.

Cranky Steve starts his response with his usual eye roll, as if we need a reminder that he doesn't want to be here. "It means you let me go first on Xbox, you let me win, you give me the cookies in your lunch, and you let me copy your homework."

Ms. Molly holds her dry erase marker inches from the board but doesn't write down what he says. Steve has managed to throw Ms. Molly off her game in a record thirty seconds. She caps the marker and taps it against her left palm.

"Okay. *Sharing.* I think that's what Steve means. Being a friend means sharing meaningful things with someone." She uncaps the marker and writes *SHARING* in big, blue letters on the board. "Marjorie? What does it mean to be a friend?"

Marjorie darts her eyes side to side. She pulls at her lip and talks in a whispery whine. "Um . . . sort of . . . well . . . places, like . . . or sometimes . . ."

"You're *mumbling,*" Cranky Steve says.

Ms. Molly caps the marker again. "Okay. This is a good example of expected and unexpected. Now, who can tell me what Marjorie did that was unexpected?"

Evan's hand flies up, and he waves it wildly while cupping his armpit with his other hand. But Cranky Steve beats him to it. "She's *mumbling.* Like I said. No one can understand her."

Evan lowers his hand and makes a pouty face.

"Steve, it's polite to wait until you're called on," Ms. Molly says. "Evan, you had your hand up?"

Evan looks surprised. "Yeah, but . . . what Steve said.

That's what I was going to say. Also, I was going to say that tomorrow me 'n' Dad are going to look for Bigfoot in the Mistral Mill Gorge because I helped him clean out his car, which was dirty because Sasquatch—that's our dog—rolled in a mud pile after it rained, and he jumped onto Dad's black leather seats, so if we find Bigfoot and he's muddy Dad said he can't sit on his leath—"

"Oh dear." Ms. Molly, who's been standing there with her jaw dropped like the rest of us, finally interrupts him. "Evan, you've gone a bit off-topic. Now, where were we?"

"Mumbling." Lenora's leaning back in her chair, balancing only on the back legs. Probably so she can get farther away from me.

"Yes, Marjorie's unexpected behavior. And what was Steven's unexpected behavior?"

"Yelling out!" Evan yells out.

"You mean like you just did, dorkface?" Steve asks.

Ms. Molly puts her hands on her hips. I wonder if she gets paid extra for this. "Steve, we do not call each other names in Friendship Group."

"Shouldn't we not call each other names *anywhere*?" Lenora points out.

"Of course. You're right, Lenora." Ms. Molly exhales. "Now, Marjorie, would you like to finish saying what it means to be a friend?"

Marjorie pulls at her fingers, shaking her head *no*. Who can blame her?

"Fine, we'll move along. Lenora?"

Lenora comes forward in her chair, landing the front legs softly on the linoleum. She taps a paper clip on the table while she thinks.

"Friendship. I think it means *sacrifice*. Like, you're willing to do something for someone, even if it's scary and uncomfortable, because your friend really needs it. Even if it breaks your dopey code." Lenora looks at me the whole time she's talking, and her eyes drill into my face.

"Why are you staring at Hyper like that? Creepy," Steve says.

Ms. Molly writes SACRIFICE on the board. "That's good. West, can you add to this list?"

I cock my head and stare right back at Lenora. Two can play at this game.

"I think being a friend means putting yourself in their shoes. Trying to *understand* them. Even if you don't like the way they can't stop bouncing their knee or making noises."

This causes Ms. Molly to flash her piano-key-sized teeth. "Very good, Westin. Understanding."

"Why should I *understand* someone who's not willing to sacrifice for me?" Lenora crosses her arms.

I cross mine back. "Because maybe this one time, Vacation Brain has flown home and is making the right decision. Maybe what you think is a fair ask is actually wrong and something you'd be totally bummed about if it actually happened. Not to mention it could get us both in a pile of trouble with a capital T—when one of us is already in a pile of trouble."

"Well, whose fault is that?" Lenora snaps.

"Fine, it's my fault. Like you said yesterday. Oh, yeah, that was really nice, by the way. You pointed out all my positive qualities, then took it back and told me how bad my brain is, just like everyone else does. Maybe I am curious and adventurous and a creative thinker. And I *also* have Vacation Brain."

Lenora is momentarily stumped. She pulls apart the paper clip and won't look at me.

"Is there something you and Lenora would like to share with the group?" Ms. Molly tilts her head.

"I know you want her back," I continue, ignoring Ms. Molly. "And I'm sorry. I really am. But it wouldn't even be her. It's wrong, and you know it."

"Easy for you to say," Lenora grumbles. "You have two parents. Ones you've known your whole life."

"Oh, sure, I know them. I know my dad never has time to talk to me, even on the phone. I know he's always disappointed in me. And I know he'd rather be with his girlfriend. At least *your* dad is interested in your life and trying to help you make friends. He even moved you to a cool farm for the fresh air."

"Are you joking?" Lenora's face gets as red as her hair. "'Cool farm'? Where your pets get murdered? At least you get to live in the house you grew up in!" she shouts.

"Not for long." I throw my hands up. "My dad doesn't give Mom enough money, so we have to move. And they're fighting over which new school to send me to, and I don't want to go to either one."

"Hey, hey, hey. What's going on with you two?" Ms. Molly asks.

Cranky Steve's eyes are wide, like he wishes he had popcorn to go with the show. Marjorie and Evan are about ready to crawl under the table.

I suck in a hard breath, feeling sweat trickle down the back of my neck. Lenora turns slightly away from me.

Ms. Molly chews on the end of her marker, probably thanking her lucky stars it's Friday. "Okay, then." She uncaps her marker and writes UNDERSTANDING on the board.

I understand all right. I understand that if I'm going

to *sacrifice* and share my magic, it certainly won't be by creating a six-inch zombie mom for a bossy, red-headed chicken farmer who bats her eyelashes at the first tiny, muscled Norse god to look her way.

FRIDAY—AT LUNCH

Josh and Snake come out of class, probably heading toward the field behind the quad. Probably going to eat lunch there. Probably not going to ask me to join them.

I lean against the outside wall by the water fountain. Maybe I shouldn't show the guys the video I took last night. Maybe I should just forget about them. Forget about Lenora. Start over. Find different friends.

"Hey," Josh says as they pass me. "Thanks, man."

"What for?" I ask.

"For not ratting us out about the football thing. That was decent," Josh says.

"Yeah," Snake mutters behind him.

Wow. Okay. Maybe they're done being mad at me

now. We are still friends. Lenora doesn't know what she's talking about. That settles it.

"I brought proof to show you guys. It's in here." I start to take my backpack off my shoulders to pull out my phone.

"I'm outta here. Going to eat by the courts." Snake takes off to the Back Five.

Josh starts to follow, so I grab his shirt. "Seriously," I whisper. "I have video."

Josh looks toward the Back Five, then back at me. "Of what?"

I tug his sleeve, pulling him toward the alcove outside of the music room, next to the upper-grade locker area.

"Dude, you're creeping me out," Josh says, yanking his sleeve away.

I unzip my backpack and take out my phone to power it up, but just then Snake calls, "Josh, man, come on. We need you for hoops!"

"No, wait," I say as Josh glances toward Snake. "It's true magic. For real. Let me show you. I wasn't kidding about the T. rex. I videoed it doing an obstacle course in my room!" The phone is fully on, and I click the video.

Josh looks at me like I just told him I wear a ballerina tutu around my house when I'm alone. "West, don't say stuff like that out loud, dude. Seriously." He shakes his head and turns away.

"No, wait!" I reach out and grab his arm.

As he tries to twist out of my grasp, my backpack slips off my shoulder, falls off my arm, and slams him right in the crotch.

Josh falls to the ground, cradling himself. "Ow, dude! You're . . . such . . . an idiot."

"Sorry. Oh, crud. I'm really sorry."

Josh flips over to his knees to catch his breath. A bunch of eighth-grade girls nearby point and giggle. He lifts himself up and glares at me.

"What's wrong with you?" Still sort of doubled over, he pushes through the wall of laughing girls and walks to the Back Five.

I angrily kick my backpack, and it flies into the shins of Zoe Fastbinder, the class president, nearly tripping her.

"Hey!" Zoe hollers. "What *is* wrong with you?"

I'm a walking disaster, *that's* what's wrong with me. I bend down to collect my pack and the papers that fell out. Zoe picks up my fire monster drawing. She shows it to her pack of girls, who all laugh.

"Aww, look at the cute little guy," Zoe says. "He's so sweet with those big eyes! Did you draw this?"

I grab it from her and shove it into my backpack.

"It's totally good. Really." She has a smirk on her face, though. "Looks like you're not inept on all levels." Her friends laugh.

This is humiliating. Popular girls watching me whack my friend in the groin, then calling my fire monster a "cute little guy." He's not little. He's not supposed to be cute. He's ferocious and fiery. He could take down the whole flipping school if he were real.

Everyone's settled eating lunch, but my appetite is completely gone. I slump down against the brick wall. Both Lenora and Josh hate me now. Totally and completely. I can imagine what Thor would say. Some sort of medieval *I-told-thou-so*. But I guess he's right.

A few minutes later, Snake walks over to get water from the fountain I'm sitting by. He ignores me, but I have an idea. While he's drinking, I pop up, press play, and slip my phone under his face.

"What the—" He jerks back.

"Look at it!" I shove it toward him. "See. A T. rex. A real, live T. rex. Running around my room."

Snake squints and dips toward my phone.

"Yup. That's right. It's real," I say.

He takes the phone to look closer. "How'd you do that? A movie app?"

"No! It's not an app. It's real."

"What's that on its back?"

"That's . . . a long story. It's sort of . . . Thor."

"Thor?" Snake looks at me like pretty much anyone would if you told them you had a tiny Scandinavian superhero riding a dinosaur in your room. But he watches the entire video. I probably have a good seven minutes of footage, with sound and everything. There's no faking it.

"Whose hand is that thing eating from?" Snake turns the screen so I can see.

"That's my hand."

"You fed a T. rex salami *from your bare hand*?" Snake's eyes go all saucer-sized.

I just shrug. "He's tame now."

"And this T. rex and those creepy army guys and . . . Thor—they just crawled out of some magic purse that belongs to your grandma?"

"It doesn't belong to . . . never mind. Yes. I can make anything I want come out of it. I mean, as long as I've seen it first. But—"

"Whatever you want?" Snake cocks his head. "So you picked these things?"

My cheeks flush. "I didn't . . . it was an accident. Like, you know the thing that made everyone scream in the tunnel yesterday?"

"That bandaged animal?"

"It wasn't an animal. It was a mummy. I made it."

"Dude." Snake thinks for a minute, then nods. "It *did* look like a mummy. Show me."

I reach into my backpack to pull out the wooden box, lifting the lid to reveal the pouch inside. Snake reaches for it, but I snap the lid shut.

"Make something then," he says.

"Hey, Snake!" Frankie calls from the Back Five. "What's taking you so long?"

Snake looks toward the courts. "Quick. Do it now."

"No. It's too dangerous here." Especially since I still haven't solved the small problem of how to make things go back. "Come over after school with the guys. I'll show you then."

"Snake, man. Come on!" Alex calls.

Snake thinks for a second. "Okay. I'll come over for five minutes. But if it's fake, I'm outta there," he says, fast-walking back toward the courts.

I run after him. "Great, cool."

"Stop following me, though," he says.

I catch up to him. "Can I shoot hoops with you guys?"

"No."

"Why not?" I ask.

"Because I like my eyes the way they are," he says, loud enough for the others to hear.

Josh throws the ball to Snake.

"But the video . . ." I say. He saw it. He believed it. Why is he being a jerk again?

"Come to show us your *magic*?" Frankie high-fives Snake, then steals the ball away and takes a shot at the net.

"I just showed Snake the video—it's a real dinosaur," I say. "Tell them, Snake."

Snake just shrugs and shoots for the basket but misses. Josh grabs the ball.

"Come on. Guys." I thrust the phone out. "Why would I lie?"

"Oh, it's not a lie. *Suuuure*, you have a dinosaur," Frankie says, trying to block Josh's shot. "Maybe you should back away slowly before you cause another basketball tragedy."

The whole group erupts with laughter, including Josh.

"It wasn't my fault Snake got hit in the face."

"Then maybe before you slam someone else in the crotch!" Alex cries, grabbing Josh's rebound. Alex and Frankie bend over laughing.

"I'm sorry about that, Josh. Really."

Alex holds the ball and shakes his head. "Dude, you seriously think *that's* the only reason why?"

"Why what?" I ask.

Frankie bumps Alex and pulls the ball out of his hands. "Why we don't want to hang out with you. How about you're annoying? How about you always have been? How about we're just not friends? Period."

I can feel it—the stinging behind my eyes. I know they can see the tears welling up.

Please don't cry, please don't cry.

But I can't help it. The waterworks have a mind of their own and turn on, pouring down my cheeks.

"Josh?"

Josh, who's been quiet in the background, stays silent. He grabs the ball from Frankie, then turns his back on me to take a shot at the basket.

I don't know what to do, so I run to the gym—the farthest I can go without leaving campus. I swing the door open and go into the dimly lit space. The bitter, gassy smell hits me in the face, but I'd rather be smelling robot farts in private than letting anyone see me cry.

I throw my backpack on the ground. Everything spills out for, like, the eleventh time today. I kick at my books and watch as the magic pouch tumbles out of the box. The pouch and my drawings slide across the smooth gym floor. They settle under the tables that have been set up for the science fair tomorrow.

I slump down against the door and have good cry. I can't do anything right. Nothing. Useless Vacation Brain.

But Alex and Frankie are wrong. Snake and Josh didn't always think I was annoying. It's only lately, after the black eye. I'm a good friend. They have no reason not to like me.

I wipe my cheeks with my sleeve and look up. A purple banner with orange letters hangs across the far end of the gym.

Science Fair Saturday
Get your science on!

That's tomorrow. I think about Alex and his who-cares fiery volcano. I hope he burns the whole smelly gym down, along with the smelly P.E. shirts.

The three-minute end-of-lunch warning bell rings. I take in a long breath. I can't go back out there and face them. Josh just stood there. He never said anything. He probably shared my password with Snake in tech class, and I *know* he let me take the fall for his paper football. Plus, he didn't believe me about T. What kind of friend is that?

Forget it. I'm not going to cry over them. They're not worth it.

I shove the wooden box into my backpack and walk across the gym floor to get the rest of my stuff, my sneakers squeaking on the brown surface. I pick up the magic pouch and scrunch it between my fingers, then sweep my drawings from the floor and carry them in a pile, my fire monster on top.

Looks like you're not inept on all levels. That's what Zoe said.

I'm not inept. Not at drawing. In fact, I'm amazing at it. Mr. Lowde even thinks so, and he's an art teacher, so he should know. This fire monster *ROCKS*. What did Mrs. Sandbeam say? *You're very talented.* Drawing *is* a talent. I may not be talented at school or enchantments, but just like Uncle Marty, I'm really good at—wait, wait, wait! *At drawing!*

Suddenly, I understand. I see it so clearly. How to control the magic—the *customized* magic. Customized for Uncle Marty's artistic talent. Just like mine. All those things in the box—the ticket, the money—Uncle Marty *drew* them.

But the instant that imaginary light bulb flickers over my head, it's outshone by a brighter, more dangerous light.

Because I just looked at my fire monster drawing. While holding the pouch.

The heat makes me drop the pouch at my feet before it burns my hand. A small—but still hot and burning—fire monster crawls out. The pouch doesn't burn, but the floor starts to. The fire monster jumps up and down and starts to roll around, sizzling.

"Dang it!" I blow at the fire monster like he's a birthday candle.

He twitches and tickles at each breath I blow, which is totally useless and doesn't work. It only makes him run away from me like we're playing tag, leaving a trail of char marks along the shiny gym floor.

"Get back here!" I yell.

The fire monster smiles as he zig-zags from me. He thinks it's a game. He darts under the science fair tables, peeking out from behind a metal leg. He grasps at the corner of the tablecloth draping down, causing fire to rip up its side. Soon, the entire tabletop is on fire.

"Shoot. No! Crud!" I grab the magic pouch and my backpack and run toward the gym door. I have to get water to douse him before he does any more damage.

I push the door open and run outside. . . . just as the explosion happens.

FRIDAY NIGHT

"What happened?" Mom opens the front door in a whirl of worry, and Dad practically shoves me into the living room. "There are a million voicemails on my phone from the school. West, what did you do? Are you okay?"

"What happened is that they think our son blew up the school gym, and you never answered your phone, so I had to leave a crazy busy workday to go to the school when he's *your* responsibility this week." Dad stays by the door because he knows Mom doesn't like him to come in.

"I was at a conference!" Mom looks from Dad to me. "You *blew up* the gym?"

I shrug. I don't know what to say. Thankfully the firefighters arrived fast enough to control the blaze, but the gym is toast. It's now four burnt walls, standing there like giant slices of charred bread. They taped the whole thing off. Other than that, the school is okay. Some classroom windows blew in, but everyone was at recess, so no one got hurt.

I still don't understand how my little fire monster could have caused such a big explosion. And if he *had* to destroy part of the school, why-oh-why couldn't it be Mr. Widelot's room?

"Westin, buddy, you can't shrug your way through this." Dad sighs. "The fire marshal grilled our son like he was one of my criminal clients, but all West will say is that he was eating lunch and then the gym blew up."

I sit on the sofa, keeping my chin down. I can't deny it. I did it. I'm probably going to jail forever.

Mom starts pacing. "How serious could this get, Phil? Oh, West." Tears come to her eyes. "You'll never get into that Waldorf school if people think you set fires."

That's what she's worried about?

I fiddle with my fingers, afraid to look up.

"Pauline, I think this proves that some nature school isn't going to help West. He needs structure—good, hard academics." Dad shakes his head at me. "You seriously have nothing to say for yourself, Westin?"

Nothing they want to hear. It's my fault. I'm trouble with a capital T. No news there.

Dad drags a hand through his hair. "We all have to be at the school tomorrow at ten a.m. The principal wants to meet with us. She's coming in, even though it's her day off." He exhales. "Not exactly how any of us want to spend a Saturday morning, I imagine, but . . . I'll see you there." He flicks a wave and marches down the front steps without closing the door.

Mom just stands there for a minute, tapping fingers against her lips, then shuts the front door. "West, talk to me. Tell me what happened."

"I-I . . . didn't mean to do anything. I don't know."

"You don't know? The gym burned down, everyone thinks you did it, and all you can say is 'I don't know'?" Mom tilts her head. "West, I want to help you, but you have to give me more than that."

There's nothing I can say. Nothing she'd believe. I shrug.

Mom exhales. "Just . . . go to your room. I need to think."

I get up and slog down the hall and into my bedroom. I don't even want dinner. Not that she's offering any.

Before I go in, Mom calls after me. "Oh, and your friend came by right after I got home."

I freeze. "What friend?"

"The Madsen boy. He said you borrowed something of his, and he needed to grab it."

"Snake was here?" I run back into the living room. "Did you let him in my room?"

Mom is sifting through mail and doesn't look up. "Hmm? Yes, I did."

"No! How could you do that?" My voice is squeaky high as I run down the hall. "I said no one could go in!"

"I was a little preoccupied listening to voicemails about you burning down the gym, West!" she calls back.

When I open my bedroom door, Thor rushes to my feet. "Ogre! He's gone! They took him!"

"What?" I look around for Tiny T.

"We tried to defend the dragon, the men and I, but there were too many for us to subdue."

"He took T? How?" I rush to my closet and look inside. Empty. Nothing under the bed either.

"Three ogres. The first came in through the big door you use. He claimed to be friend, not foe. My true warrior instinct smelled foul play, as you said there have been enemies in your ogre world. But the dragon went to him willingly, as the gentle one we have tamed him to be. We made polite conversation, and the ogre asked questions about where we came from. He seemed to know about the magic that conjured us and asked if the tools to possess it might be present. It was then that I knew he was the ogre enemy you spoke of."

"He wanted the pouch?" I slump down on my bed. This can't be happening. "Tell me everything, Thor."

"I was about to demand his departure when the other ogres came to the window."

"Other ogres? What did they look like?" I walk to my open window and look outside. There's nothing but empty lawn.

"Like you. Big, overpowering body odor. One had a very large cranial area. They referred to their leader as a serpent."

"Serpent? You mean Snake."

"Yes, that's it. The Snake threw your bedcover over the dragon and lifted him out the window to the waiting ogres. The Snake tried to take me too, but I managed to clobber his large foot, and he released me."

"Snake took the T. rex? *My* T. rex?" I slam my window shut and sit back on my bed.

"They were brutish devils, these ogre enemies of yours. But they will have theirs coming." Thor raises his mallet high. "Our dragon may have gone to them as a friend, but he will surely unleash his wrath on these unsuspecting ogres. And he grows. It will not be long before they meet their doom."

I slip off the edge of my bed to the floor. He's right. The guys have no idea what they've done. Slimy Snake's plan was probably to come in and steal the magic pouch all along. When I wasn't here and he couldn't find it, he took Tiny T.

Thor was right. Lenora too. Why would I want to be friends with brutes who would say mean things to me, leave me out, and steal my stuff? But as much as I'd love a little doom in Snake's life right now, death by dinosaur—especially one I created—isn't exactly what I imagined.

I pick up my phone and dial Snake. Amazingly, he picks up.

"Hyper, what a surprise." He laughs.

"Give him back." My voice is stern and strong.

"Hmmm, gee. Whatcha talking about?"

"My T. rex. He's not yours. Give him back."

"I don't think it's actually possible for a person to own a T. rex, is it?"

I hear hoots and howls in the background. Probably Josh, Alex, and Frankie. Snake must have me on speaker phone.

"You don't know what you've done. He's dangerous," I say.

"Dangerous?" Snake scoffs. "He came right to me, like a dog. I'll admit, he's a little feisty in his cage now, but he'll calm down."

"He nearly chewed my finger off!" a voice in the background yells. Alex. Definitely Alex.

"He's growing," I say. "He was half that size when I got him five days ago. He'll be a full-grown T. rex soon. Then what are you going to do with him?"

"If you want him back, then trade that magic pouch," Snake says.

"You don't understand. It won't work for you. It only works for one person," I say.

"Yeah, nice try. You want the dino, I want the pouch."

"Hey, find out if Josh is with him!" Alex yells out.

"With me?" I ask. "Why?"

"Alex thinks Josh blew up in the gym!" another voice yells in the background. Frankie.

"Don't be an idiot, Frankie," Snake says.

"What are you talking about?" I ask.

"Nothing. We couldn't find him after school, and he's not answering his phone. Alex is paranoid that he followed you to the gym. And then you blew him up," Snake says.

My stomach falls through the floor, into the ground, and lands somewhere in China. Josh didn't run after me, did he?

Oh, crud.

Did I blow up Josh?

No. No way. There was no one in the gym. Just me . . . well, me and a fire monster.

"I didn't blow him up," I say.

"Better not have," Snake replies. "I want that pouch tomorrow. I'll text with details. And if you tell anyone, you'll never get your dino back. I'm serious." With that, he hangs up.

I bury my face in my pillow.

I wish I could call Lenora.

SATURDAY MORNING

Having Mom and Dad together in the same room is super uncomfortable. They get weird, can't look each other in the eye, and tend to say stuff with darts attached to the words. I hate it.

Having Mom and Dad together in the same room when the room is the principal's office is even worse. Not only are they mad at each other, they're also mad at me. And usually, so is the principal.

Having Mom and Dad together in the same room when the room is the principal's office because I blew up the gymnasium . . . really, *really* sucks.

The smell of smoke and burnt wood still fills the air. Firefighters wander around the campus, inspecting the rubble. My life is over. Thrown in jail at age eleven. Before I ever get to live, hit another home run—and get back my stolen T. rex before he eats my former friends.

"Thank you for coming in on a Saturday morning. I felt this would be best done in person." Principal Peckinpaw tucks her strawberry-colored hair behind her ears. "Mr. and Mrs. . . ." She looks at my mom through her big black glasses. "I'm sorry, do you still go by Hopper?"

"She sure *does*." Dad exhales. Mom chews her lip, wringing hands in her lap.

I don't say anything, just lean against the wall, bouncing my knee up and down. There's a giant fish tank behind Principal Peckinpaw's chair, saltwater probably, filled with blue-and-yellow striped fish. Maybe the magic could turn me into a fish. I could plop into the fish tank, never to be seen again—except in fish form. At least it would be better than juvie.

"I'm sure I don't need to tell you the potential severity of this matter," the principal says. "Thankfully, no one was hurt. But it seems Westin was in the gym, and there are witnesses who claim they saw him run out yelling about a fire monster right before the explosion."

I sit there in silence. A wall clock *tick tick ticks* over my head, counting down my remaining minutes as a free man.

Principal Peckinpaw glances at me with unexpectedly soft eyes. "I'm not accusing you of anything, West. But until the fire marshal clears you, I'm afraid you'll remain suspended from school."

Dad lets out a jagged breath. "What happened to innocent until proven guilty?" He's got his lawyer hat on.

"I'm afraid it's school policy." Principal Peckinpaw pushes her glasses up her nose.

I like our principal. Even though I get sent to her office all the time, she's still nice to me, like Mr. Lowde is. She's like the Good Witch, kind but in charge, floating in to take care of all of us little people. She's always saying stuff like, "You'll get it next time, West," and "I see good in your eyes, Westin Hopper. Others will see it too."

Dad leans back in his chair and rubs his eyes. He turns to Mom. "Pauline, I can't have him next week if he's not going to school. I'm in court starting Tuesday."

"You're not the only one who works, *Phil*." Mom lowers her voice. "This is what fifty-fifty custody looks like. Remember how hard you fought for it, so you could pay less child support? Why don't you get your *nanny* to watch him?"

"Fifty-fifty is because he's my *son*," Dad bites back.

"Not to pay you less. *You* can take time off much more easily than I can. The ceiling won't cave in if you're not there. And please stop calling Cindy 'the nanny.'"

I slide farther down in my chair and feel an army of tears banging against the back of my eyes. Any minute now, waterworks.

Principal Peckinpaw holds up her hands like she does at an assembly and claps: *Bah-ba-da-bah-bah.*

I instinctively clap the response: *Bah-bah.* Mom and Dad stop mid-sentence.

"Oh, dear. Do you often fight like this in front of West?" the principal asks.

Mom and Dad look back at her with their jaws dropped.

"You know," Principal Peckinpaw says, leaning over her desk and smiling her Good Witch smile, "many children who get into trouble at school do so because there's trouble at home. What must it feel like for West to watch you speak to each other this way? He loves you both."

"Yes, well, er . . ." Dad stammers.

"I'm sure we try. . . ." Mom mumbles.

"I know it's difficult," the principal says. "But West needs you to make the effort. To be civil."

I hold my breath. No one's ever said anything like that to my parents before. Well, not in front of me anyway.

It was freaking cool. I would jump on Principal Peckinpaw and plant a wet kiss on her except:

She's not altogether sure I didn't burn down the gym.

It would be a really weird and kind of creepy thing to do.

Mom holds her hand to her mouth, her cheeks pink. "Of course. You're right."

Dad shifts in his chair, his lanky legs crunched in front of the desk. "We'll work something out for next week. Get a babysitter or something."

"Yes, sure," Mom says.

Dad pushes his chair back to stand, towering over me. His soft face disappears. "But you're not off the hook, kid." He glares at Mom. "If he set that fire—this is exactly why he needs a strict private school."

"You don't understand him." Mom exhales. "That's the last thing he needs. Don't you think he'd do better in a nurturing environment, out in nature?" She looks at the principal for support.

Principal Peckinpaw doesn't answer Mom. She sighs and looks right at me, softly. Like she's telepathically telling me she gets it. She feels sorry for me. She knows. I halfway hope it means she'll be my character witness when I go to trial. Maybe they won't send me away for life.

A moment later, the principal stands to dismiss us. On the way out, she pats my shoulder and whispers, "I'm sure this will get cleared up, West. Don't worry."

Easy for her to say. She doesn't know that:

I did start that fire.

My new best friend hates me because I won't make her a zombie mom.

My old best friend hates me too . . . except I don't know why.

I created a dinosaur that will probably grow to the size of a house and start eating people because he's so hungry.

The guys I thought were my friends will be his first meal.

Mom and Dad walk me to the parking lot. I'm in a daze, trailing a few feet behind.

"You realize how frequently he gets in trouble the weeks he's with you?" Dad says in a loud whisper. "Maybe boarding school is a better option."

"*Boarding school?* Maybe it's because he doesn't have a *father* in the house anymore." Mom's voice has a sting to it.

"Oh, that's rich, Pauline."

"Rich. Ha! We have to move because of your stingy support payments. If you spent more money caring for your son and less on your girlfriend—"

"I'm fully prepared to pay for private school. And don't bring Cindy into this!"

"I didn't bring her in. *You* did. Your private school will eat West up. He has ADHD, remember?"

"He can't use that as an excuse his whole life," Dad says.

"It's not an excuse!" Mom throws her hands up. "It's a disability, Phil. Asking him to just try harder is like asking a blind kid to try to see."

They think they're whisper-arguing, but they're lousy at it. I put my hands up to my ears to block it out. I wish I could disappear, so they wouldn't fight over me anymore. And that's when I see him—my fire monster. He's lurking around the corner of a cement wall by the parking lot, trying not to touch anything.

"I'll be right back." My parents are too busy arguing to hear me.

I zip over to where he's hiding and crouch down. "You're alive. I thought you died in the explosion."

The fire monster looks up at me with giant, puppy-dog eyes and a what-the-heck-just-happened expression. I guess he is pretty adorable . . . for a havoc-wreaking creature.

"You got me in a heap of trouble, you know." I look around to make sure none of the firefighters or police officers are lurking. The last thing I need is to be seen playing with fire. "How'd you cause such a huge explosion anyway?"

He just shrugs his fiery shoulders. I can't be mad at him. After all, I made him. And I understand more than anyone about doing bad stuff without meaning to.

I slip my backpack off my shoulders and pull out the wooden box. Lifting the lid, I adjust the opening of the pouch inside. "Can you get back in here without burning the box or my backpack or me or any more of the school?"

Please, please go in. Don't pull a T. rex on me.

The fire monster nods quickly, waves goodbye, and, in a spark, slips into the pouch.

I glance down. A wisp of smoke wafts up from the edge of the box, but nothing else is toasted. *Phew!* But I can't help wondering: the croc, the owl, the mummy, and now the fire monster . . . they all went back. So why won't Tiny T?

Is Thor right? Am I supposed to get enlightenment from him or something?

So far, the only enlightening has been of the school gym.

I peek around the corner at Mom and Dad. Mom sits in her car, waiting for me. Dad is standing on the opposite side of the parking lot, near the driver's side door of the Evidence.

My phone pings as I walk to him. I look at the screen, and my stomach squeezes. It's from Snake.

If u ever want to see ur lizard alive, bring the pouch. My house. Rec room over garage. 2 p.m. today. No grown-ups or else.

"Everything okay?" Dad asks as I walk up. "You're turning green."

I nod, staring at the screen. They wouldn't kill him. Would they? At least I know T hasn't killed *them*—yet.

Dad kisses the top of my head. "I'll see you tomorrow afternoon, okay?"

Tomorrow afternoon. I'm running out of time. I have to figure out a way to get T back—and return him to the Other Realm—before I go to Dad's.

"Can you wait here a second, Dad? Don't move."

I dash over to Mom's car and tap on her window. I roll my finger so she'll open it.

"Get in the car, West." She sighs. "I have a lot to do today."

"Dad wants to take me right now. You know, save you from having to drop me at his house tomorrow."

I know this lie will work for two reasons:

Mom hates talking to Dad, especially after they've been fighting, so she won't check my story.

She'd probably rather not see my face for the rest of the day anyway.

Mom exhales. "Really, he said that?" She looks over in Dad's direction, and he actually waves back, helping me without even knowing it. "What about your homework? Your planner?"

"I have my stuff." I point to my backpack. I'm probably banished from school anyway, but I don't remind her of that.

"All right." Mom rolls up her window. Then she rolls it back down. "Wait. Gimme a kiss." She sticks her cheek out, and as I lean in to kiss her, she reaches up to hug me. "What am I going to do with you?" She squeezes me tightly.

I squeeze her back, then run over to Dad, who's now sitting in his car. Time for lie number two. I feel bad about it, but Tiny T's life—and possibly my former friends' lives—are at stake. And if Tiny T gets *really* huge before I can send him back to the Other Realm, then *everyone's* lives are at stake. Lying is a small price to pay.

"Mom wants you to drop me off at a friend's house," I tell Dad, opening the passenger-side door. "It's for a school project."

"So she just left you?" Dad lets out a long breath. "All right, get in."

I slip into the front seat and toss my backpack by my feet. I need help. And there's only one place I might get it. I just hope she'll see me.

SATURDAY—LATER

The wheels on Dad's car spin up dust from the long dirt driveway that leads to Lenora's yellow farmhouse. I hop up the front steps while Dad waits in the driveway.

"Is Lenora home?" I ask Grannie once she opens the squeaky old front door.

Grannie wipes the sweat off her neck with her apron front and yells up the stairs. "Nora! Company!" She turns and heads into the house. "Come in, son. Go on up."

I turn and wave at my dad from the porch. A moment later, he and the Evidence disappear around a bend under the arch of oak tree branches. I step across the threshold and stop. The house smells like chicken soup. Hopefully not made with one of Lenora's pets.

"Westin, right?" Lenora's dad pops his head through the kitchen door. "Nice to have you back!"

"Thanks, Mr. Pickering."

"That's Ned, remember. What are you kids up to today? Saddle up the horses maybe?"

I look up the stairs, wondering if Lenora's coming down. "Um . . ."

"Course not," he says. "You kids don't want to hang out on a farm. Need a ride somewhere? Downtown, the mall?"

"Yes—probably. Could you drop us somewhere?"

"Sure, sure. Just holler."

"Is Lenora . . .?" I point upstairs.

"Nora!" her dad shouts up the stairs. "You hear Grannie? Your friend is here."

I hear foot clomps and a pair of legs appear at the mid-landing of the stairs. Lenora bends down to see who's at the door.

"Oh. You. Heard of a phone?" She turns on her heels and walks back up the stairs.

Mr. Pickering grimaces. "Uh-oh. Looks like you've met the wrath of Queen Nora. Don't worry, son, she's softer than she seems."

I stand there, not sure what to do.

"Geez, come on up already!" Lenora yells down.

I climb the stairs and walk down a dark hall. The walls are dingy white, and the four doors on either side are painted green. They're all closed, except for the last one on the right. I head there and peer in. Lenora is sitting on the blue carpet next to her bed, folding a pile of clothes.

"What's up?" She doesn't bother looking up.

I go in and stand beside her, not sure what to do. Lenora's room is super clean and tidy and surprisingly girly. White lace drapes let the sun peek through, a mirror with a gold frame hangs on one wall, and a painting of kittens peeking out of a basket is over the bed.

I shake my head. Her grannie must have decorated this or something.

On the bedside table is a framed photo of two grown-ups. I recognize the man—Lenora's dad. The woman has copper hair, like Lenora's. That must be her mom. Next to that is a photo of Lenora hugging a white chicken that I assume is—was—Bobbie.

I unzip my backpack and take out the wooden box, my sketchbook and pencils, and Uncle Marty's drawings, which I packed this morning before leaving. Lenora doesn't stop folding.

"I need your help," I say.

"Yeah?" She says with a *who cares?* tone, picking up a red sock and a blue one and folding them together.

I pull out my phone to show her the ransom text. "Snake broke into my room yesterday and took Tiny T."

"Whoa. What?" Lenora finally stops and looks at me.

"You were right about them—all of them. Except I don't think Josh was with them. I think it was Snake, Alex, and Frankie."

"Still defending Josh?" Lenora shifts her knees under her and keeps folding socks.

"No. It's just that . . . he's missing."

"Missing?"

"The guys don't know where he is. They think he might have followed me into the gym." I look down. "Before it exploded. But he didn't."

"Wait, you were in the gym?"

"Long story. I was holding a drawing of this fire monster that I made last weekend in one hand and the pouch in the other and—"

"Holy fire monster! *You* caused the explosion?"

I take in a big breath. "Maybe?"

Lenora throws a hand over her mouth, her eyes bugging out like a gecko's. Then she shrugs and laughs. "The gym smelled funny anyway."

I'm glad she's laughing, but it's so *not* funny. "True, but I'm in big trouble. It did give me an idea, though."

I splay Uncle Marty's drawings across the floor. "Remember these?"

"Yeah . . . your uncle's drawings, right?"

"Exactly. His *drawings*. What if the magic was customized to his talent? You conjure with the eye, right? You have to be able to see it first. If Uncle Marty *drew* something, then he could *see* it. I think I can do the same thing."

Lenora twists her lips. "Let me get this straight. You think you can draw it, then look at the drawing, and that will count as conjuring with the eye? Have you tested it yet?"

"Beyond accidentally bringing a fire monster to life, you mean?" I shake my head. "I've been a little too busy getting in trouble. And I wanted to run the theory by you."

She folds a shirt and puts it on the pile. "Well, I guess you should try drawing something—but something that can't wander off, attack anyone, grow taller than a tower, or cause general mayhem."

I glance down. "So, something . . . not alive. Or that was *ever* alive?" I try to say it gently.

Lenora exhales, fortunately not in a stormy kind of way. "Look, I was thinking . . . about everything you said in Friendship Group. And you were right."

"I was?" That's gotta be a first.

"It was amazing to think, for a minute, that I could meet her. You know? But it would never be my real mom."

"Yeah. I'm super sorry. I wish you still had your mom. Maybe you could make your dad talk about her? I mean, talking to Gram about Uncle Marty went better than we thought it would. And you can talk to me about your mom anytime. Anything you want to say, even if it's not true."

Lenora narrows her eyes. "So, like, if I say she was an astronaut?"

"I'll ask what it was like on the moon."

"And if I say she was a pirate?"

"I'll help you look for the treasure!"

Lenora smiles softly. "You're a good guy." Then she pushes my shoulder. "Anyway, if you think you can draw magic, we probably don't need to hunt for treasure."

I wag a colored pencil. "Good point."

"And while I'm groveling . . ." She looks down. "I'm sorry for all those crappy things I said after the field trip. About your brain and self-control. I know you don't mean half the stuff you do. I *do* understand."

"Aw, shucks. Ms. Molly would be proud."

"Anyway, you made me realize that I have stuff to be grateful for. Like my dad. And meeting you. Even if I have to live on this smelly farm."

The tips of my ears are practically burning off my head. It's weird having a *real* friend. Lenora says whatever is on her mind, the fiery stuff and the kind stuff too.

"Are your parents really gonna make you move and go to some other school?" she asks. "That would be terrible."

I exhale. "I don't know."

"Well, I hope not. Who wants to lose a friend just when they figured out their magic?"

We chuckle, and Lenora stretches out a hand. "Forgiven?"

"Totally." I put down the pencil and shake it. "So, should we see if I'm right?" I point to my art stuff.

"What are you going to make?"

I start drawing, fast and furious. "Don't look. It's a surprise."

Lenora rolls her eyes and goes back to folding.

When I finish, I reach for the pouch, look at the drawing, and hold my breath. If this doesn't work, then I won't have to worry about whether I'm jailed for burning the gym down—eventually my pet T. rex will eat the jail.

In a flash, the pouch has a lump inside.

"It worked!" I exclaim.

Lenora's eyes go wide. "Let's just hope it's what you drew and not an alien shark. I mean, it's . . . not an alien shark. Right?" She inches back.

I pull out the lump to inspect, smile, and toss it to her. "Inspired by our very own Mr. Widelot."

Lenora catches it. "A tiny T-shirt?" She reads the words on it:

MY FRIEND BLEW UP THE SCHOOL GYM AND ALL I GOT WAS THIS STINKIN' SHIRT

She shakes her head. "You're such a dork. But hey, maybe one of my chickens can wear it." She sets it down.

"This is awesome!" I exclaim.

"Indeed," Lenora agrees. "But even if you can control the magic by drawing, how are we going to rescue Tiny T?"

"With a little help from some friends," I say.

"Bad news, dude. Last time I checked, we didn't have any."

"We have a customized magic pouch and colored pencils. We can make some!" I raise a pencil.

I'm not exactly sure how to draw my idea, so I take out my phone to search the internet for Viking-era photos. Then I lie down on my stomach, flattening out the sketchpad on the blue carpet. This is a big drawing job, so I settle in.

I chew on my bottom lip and start sketching, outlining shapes of weapons and warriors with the black pencil. The soft sound of pencil lightly scritch-scratching the paper is the only thing I hear.

After a few minutes, I prop myself up on my elbow to get a better view and show the initial drawing to Lenora.

"Oh, wow. That's awesome. But, uh, kind of risky, right? What if you can't get rid of them after?"

"If it doesn't work, then getting rid of them will be the least of our troubles. A hungry T. rex ravaging the countryside, having eaten our classmates, will be way worse."

"Maybe we should tell a grown-up or something?" she says.

I point to the ransom text. "It says no grown-ups or else." My lips curl to a frown. "Anyway . . . can you imagine? *Hey, Mom and Dad, I know I'm suspended from school for possibly burning the gym down, but my former friends stole my live T. rex and are holding him as ransom for Uncle Marty's magic pouch that I took from Gram's basement. Can you help?*"

Lenora puts her hand on my shoulder. "Point taken. Now what?"

"We go get Thor. Will your dad drive us?"

"Totally." She folds the last shirt and pops up. "Let's go. We have a wingless dragon to rescue."

It feels good to have Lenora not angry at me anymore.

It'll feel even better if this plan to get Tiny T back actually works.

SATURDAY AFTERNOON

Lenora's dad pulls his pickup truck onto my street. He agrees to park a few houses away—so Mom won't see—and wait there. He doesn't even ask why. He's that chill.

When I go into the house, Mom is sitting on the sofa with a bag of potato chips in her lap and the TV turned on to some show with people crying and talking. She pops up as I walk in.

"Is everything okay? Why aren't you with your father?"

"I forgot my math homework." I run past her toward my room.

"Oh." She goes back to watching her show.

In my room, Thor is sitting on my desk. The army men are on the floor at his feet.

"Ogre, you have returned!" Thor exclaims. "We feared perhaps you had been hauled to the dungeon for the fiery destruction you caused."

"Not yet." I set my backpack down on the floor next to the men.

"Have you found the dragon?"

I nod. "Sort of. Lenora requests your presence. She's waiting outside with a mission."

"If my lady commands, it shall be so. With what duty am I to be charged? Is there a two-headed serpent that needs slaying?"

"In a way. It's a mission to rescue our dragon from Snake."

Thor hefts his hammer. "I am an expert in battling snakes!"

I pull out the drawing I made at Lenora's and explain the plan to Thor.

"You etched me an army?" he asks. "The likeness is exceptional. It is a fine piece of artwork. We shall prevail!"

I pull a gym bag from the shelf in my closet and empty a smelly shirt and old underwear from inside. "Climb in here."

Thor leans his head into the opening. "The aroma in

your fabric carriage is most unpleasant," he says as he climbs in. I bet it is.

"You have to be really, really quiet. I'll try not to jostle you," I say into the hole. I take the pouch out of the box so it won't knock Thor on the head and place it in the gym bag with him.

I hoist the strap over my shoulder for support. Even though Thor is only about a foot high, he's pretty muscular—plus he's carrying his hammer. The bag weighs *a lot*. I'm surprised I can lift it.

I nod goodbye to Mom, hoping she doesn't fire up the copter and get curious about why the bag I'm hauling to Dad's looks like it's squirming. Thankfully, she's too into her TV show to care. I trod up the street and hoist myself into Ned's truck, setting the gym bag at my feet.

"Did he say yes?" Lenora asks quietly.

I nod and open the gym bag just a bit, so Lenora can see.

"My lady!" Thor's little voice booms out the hole. "The blue of your eyes is—"

I stick my hand over the opening, panicked, and glance at her dad. Thank goodness for that loud truck engine.

Lenora laughs.

I give Ned the address, and he drives us to Snake's

house. The street is covered in potholes, causing Lenora to lean into me as the truck dips and rises. The butterflies in my stomach are in an epic battle, like the one I'm about to be in myself. What if the guys already hurt T? Or the reverse?

"Pull up here, please. That's the one, over there." I point to a brown house with a basketball hoop over the garage. I look at the window over the hoop. I know that's where they are. It's Snake's rec room. I've been in there a million times. Okay, well maybe not a million. But definitely a few.

Lenora and I climb out of the truck, and she grabs one handle of the gym bag to help me steady it.

"Can you wait for us, Dad?" Lenora asks.

"How long are you going to be?" Ned asks through his bushy mustache.

"I don't know. Not long," she says.

"Sure thing. Maybe I'll sit back and get a little shut eye then. Won't need to bang on the door to get you though, right?" He winks, turns off the truck engine, and leans back. He starts snoring before we even shut the car door.

"Are you scared?" Lenora asks as we head to the staircase at the back of the garage.

I'm totally scared out of my mind, but I say, "Nah. You?"

"Nah." Lenora looks around. "Sort of."

I peek around the garage to the backyard. No sign of anyone. "Come on. Up here." I climb the stairs holding the gym bag from the bottom. Lenora follows.

A trail of sweat dribbles down my back under my jersey, even though it's a cold day. I'm trying super hard to be careful with Thor, but I trip on a stair and he grunts loudly. The door swings open right away, and Frankie sticks his big melon head out.

"Well, well. Hyper. Right on time."

Lenora and I go in, setting the gym bag down behind the sofa. The room looks just like I remember it. There's a giant TV on an old, tall dresser, a foosball table, beanbag chairs, and a soda machine that makes a loud buzzing noise.

And right in the center, Alex and Snake stand beside a raccoon cage—with an angry T. rex inside.

"Why'd you bring your girlfriend?" Alex giggles.

"She's not my girlfriend, Alex."

"What's in the bag?" Snake nods toward the sofa.

"It's to carry the T. rex home." I say. "And I brought the ransom."

Poor T starts banging wildly inside his cage. I hope he hasn't hurt himself. The cage is way too small. He's about to bust the sides. And I can tell he's bigger. He must have grown overnight. Ooh, he's mad, shoving his shoulders against the grated sides, thwacking his tail on the cage floor.

I take a step toward him, but Snake stands in front of the cage, blocking me. "Nuh-uh," he says. "Not until you hand over the magic."

"Is he okay?" I ask, trying to see around Snake.

"*He's* fine. But he nearly ate my freaking hands off getting him in that cage," Frankie says. "I don't know why you'd want him, anyway. He's a violent killer."

"Shut it, Frankie." Snake darts him a look, then turns back to me. "Just give me the pouch and you can take your dinosaur."

"It's in here. I'll get it." I kneel by the sofa, keeping my back to the guys, and unzip the gym bag. As soon as it's open a crack, Thor pops his head out.

"You okay?" I whisper.

He flashes me his newly learned thumbs-up.

I nod at Lenora, signaling her that it's time to distract the guys. Then I pull out the magic pouch and look at my drawing.

Here we go. Moment of truth.

Lenora takes a step forward. "Why'd you lizard-brains have to steal the T. rex, anyway?" she asks. "West would've given you anything you wanted from the pouch. He only wanted to be your friend."

"I don't need friends who can't even catch a basket-ball," Snake says.

"Dude, are you serious?" Lenora asks. "Can't you see how bad he feels about it? So you got a black eye. Are you that much of a baby?"

Frankie and Alex laugh, and Snake shushes them fast. "I'll give you two minutes to hand over the magic," he says to me.

In my hand, the pouch bulges, and suddenly an army of six-inch Vikings with spears, bows and arrows, clubs— I even drew a catapult—marches out behind the sofa.

My jaw drops. You'd think I'd be used to the magic by now, but it's still mind-bending. I did it!

Lenora continues. "Why keep blaming West for not catching the ball, anyway? Maybe you could try catching your *own* ball sometime."

Alex and Frankie snicker.

Out of view from the guys, Thor assembles the Vikings by weapon. "Welcome, warrior." He holds the pouch open, shaking the hand of a hulky, bearded guy with a horned helmet and a two-sided ax. "Ax-men to the left."

The Viking bows deeply and moves left, behind the sofa. Another warrior—this time a scrawny Viking with a metal helmet and nose plate—emerges from the pouch.

Poor dude. I should've drawn him beefier.

"That's a fine sword and shield you carry there," Thor says.

The little Viking falls to one knee. "Almighty Thor. To follow you into battle is the honor of a lifetime." He looks up, trembling with a mixture of fear and awe. "I shall not fail you."

"One minute left." Snake tries to ignore Lenora, but it's clear he's getting mad. "Or we keep the T. rex."

"Keep him?" Lenora scoffs. "Good luck with that. He's growing, you turds. Where are you going to keep a full-grown T. rex?"

Finally, the last warrior comes out—on horseback.

"A beast! You have outdone yourself, ogre," Thor says as I hide the magic pouch back in the gym bag.

"Come on already!" Snake shouts. "What's taking so long?"

"What's wrong, is your mommy calling?" Lenora asks.

Thor addresses his hoard of pint-sized Vikings in a hushed roar behind the sofa. "Around this cloth carriage stands a serpent demon disguising himself as a boy. We shall take him down, rescue the dragon, and above all, keep the fairest maiden in all the land safe from harm."

The men grunt.

"To battle!" Thor raises his mallet high and charges

around me, followed by his army of six-inch Vikings, a catapult, and a mini horse.

"Enough. Let's get this ov—what the—" Snake jumps when he sees the little Vikings run out.

Thor, who is more than twice the size of his tallest Viking, leads the ax- and swordsmen, screaming and howling, as they rush toward the boys.

"Holy crud!" Eyes large, Alex jumps behind Frankie at the sight of the army. They both back away.

"You can't be serious," Snake says. "All I have to do is step on them!"

He raises his foot, and I gulp. I didn't think of that. But before his foot comes down, a cluster of toothpick-sized spears launch from the Vikings and stick Snake in the leg.

Snake doubles over, grabbing his thigh with one hand and yanking at the tiny spears with the other. "Ouch! They speared me!"

"That's gotta hurt, Snake. You okay?" Frankie asks as he ducks behind the TV.

"Get over here and help me!" While Snake tugs at the spears, the Viking on horseback circles him at a gallop, tying thick twine around Snake's ankles.

"You go, Alex." Frankie pushes Alex toward Snake.

"Nuh-uh." Alex runs back to safety behind the TV.

The Vikings easily spot the hiding place. The catapult launches the soldiers into the air, and they land on the top of the TV by Alex and Frankie's heads.

In seconds, the Vikings are shooting arrows—with twine attached—up and over the hanging lights. They begin swinging at the boys' heads. *Whoosh!* They kick them in the ears and thump their foreheads with metal shields.

The boys duck and swat at the tiny Vikings, their fists cracking against the armor with each pass. *Thwack!*

The Vikings are not deterred. The archers step close and launch flaming arrows into the air. They land at all different points on Alex's and Frankie's clothes, erupting in pockets of smoke.

"I'm on fire!" the twins screech. They bat at each other, trying to put out the flames, which have set off the squeal of the smoke detector overhead.

With the guys otherwise occupied, Lenora and I hurry to Tiny T. We try to lift the raccoon cage, but it's too heavy, and T keeps swiping at us through the grate.

At that moment, Snake manages to free an arm from the scrawny Viking trying to bind his hands. But with his ankles tied together, he has nowhere to go. Snake begins to topple over and reaches out, pulling Lenora down with him. She smacks her knees down on the floor.

"Ow!" Lenora tries to wriggle free of Snake's grip. "Let go of me!"

I jump up to help her, but my shirt gets caught on the corner of the cage. "Thor, help!" I yell, trying to yank free.

Thor has had enough. The Vikings recapture Snake's arm with their ropes, and Thor climbs up onto the bully's chest. A lightning bolt zaps the carpet by Snake's head.

Thor raises his hammer, ready to smack Snake across the nose. "Unhand her at once, you serpent demon!"

Snake's eyes go wide, and he finally lets go.

I twist my shirt loose and rush over to pull Lenora up. "You okay?"

Lenora nods and brushes her knees off. "Thanks. You too, Thor."

Thor's face is as red as Lenora's hair—no one messes with his lady. He bows deeply while the rest of the Vikings finish tying up Snake and the boys.

Lenora and I turn back to the cage, and I reach to open the door.

"Don't open it!" Lenora cries in unison with the guys.

"No, it's fine. He's tame. You okay, boy?" I reach in to pet Tiny T, but he lunges and hisses at me. I pull my hand away in time and snap the door closed.

"Tame?" Snake laughs. "You're delusional."

"That thing wanted to claw my eyeballs out," Frankie shouts.

"Yeah, good riddance," Alex adds.

I slowly open the cage door and extend my hand again. "It's okay, buddy. It's me."

Tiny T sniffs hesitantly. Then he rushes out and lunges at me.

Lenora screams, and the boys' eyes go wide. "He's gonna eat Hyper!" Frankie yells.

T jumps onto my lap, and for a second it seems he might chow my face, but instead he rubs his forehead against my chin.

Snake momentarily stops his thrashing on the ground to watch while T licks my face and cuddles. Alex and Frankie drop their jaws.

"The T. rex is, like, *hugging* him!" Alex exclaims.

"How come he didn't do that with us?" Frankie whines. "Lucky!"

The Vikings finish pinning Snake's arms and legs, and Thor stands on his chest, triumphant. "We have subdued the giant serpent disguised as a boy, along with his lackeys."

"Get him off me!" Snake shouts. "Let me up."

"Not a chance." I set Tiny T down beside me and stand up. "Thor, are they secure?"

Tiny T saunters slowly over to where Snake lies and bares his fangs. Dino drool drips onto Snake's forehead.

"Get it away!" Snake screeches. "He's going to eat me!"

I laugh and let Snake squirm for a second before hoisting T up.

Thor does a quick walk around the boys, kicking at the ropes. "All good, ogre."

"Okay. The men can go home."

Lenora takes the magic pouch out of the gym bag, and Thor lifts open its edge. One by one, the Vikings crawl back into the pouch, dragging their catapult and weapons with them.

"Fine job. Thank you, soldier. You did well." Thor pats each of them on the back as they go in. But he stops the little scrawny one, the one who allowed Snake's arm to get free. "You mustn't let your mind wander in battle. Your slight caused my lady harm."

The tiny Viking bows his head. "Her hair," he says. "I was entranced. She is a goddess of epic proportions."

Thor scowls. "Never mind her hair." The tiny Viking trembles, and Thor eases up. "But you are correct. It is easy to lose oneself in her beauty. Carry on." Thor ushers him in as Lenora blushes. I shake my head.

"Dude!" Snake pleads. "We were just joking. Come on."

"Yeah, this is nuts. Untie us," Alex says.

I ignore them and bend down by the magic pouch, holding Tiny T in my arms. "How about you, buddy? You ready to go back to the other world?"

Thor holds the pouch open, looking hopeful. I'm not sure what I expect, since T would hardly fit in there now anyway, but he doesn't make a move.

I sigh. "Okay. Well, I gotta at least put you in this gym bag. Just for a little while."

T struggles at first but settles down when Thor hops in with him.

"You can't just leave us here all tied like this!" Snake shouts.

"Yeah, I can," I say. "Good luck explaining it to your parents. And if you try to blame it on me, I'll use my magic to fill your room with spiders."

I wouldn't. But they don't know that.

Lenora and I hoist up the much heavier gym bag and start to walk out.

"But we're friends, man. Friends play jokes on each other. We're even now. You know, for the basketball," Snake says.

I stop and turn. Not long ago, I would've died to hear Snake say those words. Now I know better.

"That's funny for three reasons," I say. "One: I never meant to hurt you. I didn't space out during basketball to be mean. I have ADHD, and sometimes I can't help stuff. The stuff you do to me—it's mean. Plain old mean. Two: Alex was right yesterday. We're actually *not* friends. Not at all. And three: Lenora's right too. Next time, try catching the ball yourself—with your hands instead of your face."

Alex and Frankie snort, and Snake shouts, "If you walk out of here, we'll never talk to you ever again! You'll have no friends!"

"I don't want friends like you." I smile at Lenora. "I want friends like her. She's way better than all of you combined."

SATURDAY–BACK
AT MOM'S HOUSE

Ned drives us back to my house and drops us off. When Lenora and I walk in, Mom is basically in the same spot I left her before, munching chips and watching sappy shows. She sits up. "You're back again? Is everything okay?"

"Long story. Mom, this is Lenora. She's a friend from school."

Lenora smiles and waves at Mom. Then we walk straight past, carrying the heavy gym bag, as Mom scrunches the potato chips closed and stands up. We have to move quickly. All we need is for Tiny T to start thrashing and catch Mom's attention.

"Wait. Are you sleeping here or Dad's tonight?" Helicopter launching, stand clear.

"Sleeping here." Lenora and I leave the room.

"He could've called. Why the change? And what are you two doing with that bag?" Mom calls after us. "Have you eaten?"

"It's for a school project!" I call back down the hall. Hopefully the mention of school, combined with Mom's sappy shows, will keep her distracted.

Lenora and I bolt into my room, close the door, and set the gym bag on my sizzled baseball carpet. Thor calls out from inside the gym bag: "May we be relieved of this aromatic cloth carriage now?"

I unzip it, and he pokes his head out.

"Thanks for your help, Thor. We couldn't have done it without you," Lenora says.

"My lady, is the sun shining brighter in the kingdom today, or am I mistaking the glow for the beauty emanating from your hair, the color of warm embers?"

"Gotta love this guy." Lenora smooths her apparently ember-colored hair. "Here, let me help you out." She reaches in to lift him out of the bag, and his rugged face turns a little pink.

"What about T?" I tug the side of the opening.

"He isn't well," Thor says. "He barely moved during transport. I believe the stress from his captivity with the serpent ogres may have taken his last bit of strength."

I reach in and pet Tiny T's side. He's cool to the touch and taking shallow breaths.

Lenora peeks over my shoulder. "T doesn't look so good."

"Without proper dragon sustenance, he is not long for this world. He must return to the Other Realm forthwith," Thor says.

My stomach squeezes. It's my fault T is here, basically starving, despite the piles of deli meat. He doesn't deserve to die. I lift him out of the pouch. He's limp and heavy.

"Thor is right. He needs real dinosaur food. We have to send him back right away."

T's chest rises and falls quickly. I stroke his leathery skin. I never meant for this to happen. He looks so weak. It reminds me of the day Gram's dog died. He could only lie there, breathing heavily, as we petted his wiry fur and told him it would be okay—until he took his last breath. I don't want that to happen to Tiny T.

"I'm sorry, little guy. I'll try to send you home."

Lenora kneels by me and places her hand next to mine on T's side. He lets out a small groan, and she flinches. T tries to lift his head, but he doesn't have the strength.

"Please don't die," she says.

"I've got to do this fast. I hope it works." I reach for my sketchpad and pencils and begin drawing. Lenora sits cross-legged, holding the magic pouch in her lap, stroking Tiny T's head. She has tears in her eyes.

Thor climbs up onto her and sits down on her thigh. "What is the ogre doing?" Thor asks.

"His talent," Lenora replies.

I draw and erase and draw some more for nearly ten minutes. I draw exactly what I want to have happen: Tiny T putting his leg in the pouch. I put on the final touches, tear the drawing off the sketchpad, and hand it to Lenora.

"What do you think?" I ask, tapping the pencil against my leg.

"It's super good," she replies. "Let's just hope that once T sticks his toe in the pouch, the rest of him will follow."

I take the pouch in my hand. After a good, hard look at my drawing, I toss the pouch to the center of my room—before Vacation Brain has a chance to make five more Tiny T friends to gobble us all up.

T is still flat on his back. Nothing happens.

"It's not working." I jiggle my knees.

"Maybe he just doesn't have the energy," Lenora suggests.

I tap my sketchpad on my knee like a drum. "Come on, T. You gotta get up."

Maybe I have to draw a Tiny T energy drink . . . coffee or something. I chew on the end of my pencil, thinking, when the headless men suddenly stand at attention and begin marching in formation. Tiny T lifts his head, then his body, and then, finally, he stands.

"Ah, the beast has arisen!" Thor says.

Lenora leaps up on the bed and starts jumping. "Come on, T! You've got this!"

Tiny T roars a tiny dinosaur roar and clambers past me toward the pouch on the floor. My heart pulses in my neck.

"The ogre's artistic strength appears satisfactory to the task!" Thor exclaims.

"Go, T!" Lenora cheers him on.

At the sound of her voice, T stops and cocks his head in that cute way—well, okay, it was cute when he was the size of a squirrel.

"Crud." Lenora's voice is squeaky high. "Shoo, T. Keep going."

Thor holds his mallet at the ready. I get up and position myself between Lenora and Tiny T—just in case.

"Time to go home, T. Thanks for being such a cool dinosaur. I know what you came here to teach me, okay? Not just about magic . . . but that I'm not only about the trouble I get into. That I have positives too. Like the imagination that brought you here in the first place. And the curiosity to figure out how to send you home. And the creativity to draw it right."

I look at Lenora. "And what a friend looks like. Even if you had to eat half my room before I figured it out."

Just then, Mom knocks on the door. "West? What was that sound? Did you bring an animal in that bag?"

T hears her voice and turns toward the door. He swishes his tail and takes a lumbering step back toward the center of the room.

"Don't come in, Mom!"

"I know I promised, but that sounded like a—" Mom starts to open the door.

"Go, quick!" I yell, waving my arms.

There's no way this is going to work. T is like a bull-dog trying to get into a lady's purse. Mom is going to see him, and I'm pretty sure if she knows I'm magicking up dinosaurs in my bedroom, my newly mastered magic pouch will get a permanent time-out.

But then T tucks his foot into the pouch, and just as Mom enters the room . . .

He's gone.

Lenora is on my bed, I'm in front of her, both our mouths open wide enough to catch flies. Thor hides behind Lenora's leg, and the army men freeze in place.

Mom stands with her hands on her hips and surveys my room. "Westin Scott Hopper—your room! What happened to your carpet? And your desk?" She walks over to the desk, charred from Thor's lightning bolts, and runs her finger along the marks.

"I'm . . . not done cleaning?" I say, still in shock.

"Not done?" Mom is furious. "You haven't even started! Considering you're being accused of arson and there are burn marks everywhere, playtime with your friend is over. You can spend the rest of the day cleaning this room, and it had better be done by morning. Lenora, can you get your mom to pick you up?"

Lenora shrugs. "Mom died. But my dad can come get me."

"Oh." Mom's face falls. "You're *that* friend? I'm so sorry. I guess . . . you can stay a little longer." She turns on her heels and walks to the door.

Whoa, I don't think I've ever seen the copter decelerate that fast. But then she revs it up for one last flyover.

"But clean this up, West. Immediately. I mean it. Clothes put away, bed made, nothing on the floor." She leaves without shutting the door.

I walk to the pouch and stand over it. "He's gone," I say in quiet disbelief.

Lenora stays on the bed, next to Thor. "Yeah, it worked. Whaddaya know?"

I look over at her. "Did you really just use the 'my mom died' card to keep me out of trouble?"

Lenora smirks. "Yeah. I know how to *sacrifice* for friends."

I raise a brow.

Thor bends at the waist, bowing to Lenora. "My lady, I deeply regret the loss of your mother. I do not feel right returning to the Other Realm if you are grieving."

Lenora kneels. "I need to take care of this one myself, Thor." She glances at me. "It's time to talk to my dad. About my mom." She looks back at Thor. "But you've been very good to me, and I appreciate your concern."

Thor bows. "I would climb a mountain of fire for you, my lady."

"I'm sure." She sits up. "West, do you have scissors?"

"Sure." I grab a pair from my desk. "What for?"

Lenora clasps a long lock of hair at the nape of her neck and clips. "A gift." She hands it to Thor. It's twice as long as he is.

Thor takes an end and falls to one knee. "My lady, this will make the finest cord once braided. And with it, I shall scale the tallest fortress, lasso the finest steed, pull the richest treasure from the sea. And I shall have you with me, always."

Lenora giggles. "Here, I'll help you braid it."

Thor holds one end while Lenora braids, and I sit on my floor to sketch: Thor, walking into the pouch, holding a cord of red, braided hair, followed in a line by an army of headless green men.

And since I figure it's okay to use magic to clean up a mess that magic—*mostly*—made, in the background, my room is spotless. The charred marks on my rug and desk are gone. My clothes are hung perfectly in my closet, un-torn by T. rex claws.

Lenora wraps the braid around and around and fastens it to Thor's belt. I hold up the drawing when I'm done. "Guess it's time for you guys to go too," I say.

Thor bows to Lenora, climbs off the bed, marches to my side, and punches me in the arm.

Ouch. That actually hurt.

"Ogre." Thor nods.

"Thor," I reply. "Thanks. For babysitting my dinosaur this week. And you know, battling the serpent ogres. And stuff."

"You are most welcome for all the *stuff*, ogre." Thor winks and lifts his hand in the air. I high-five his little palm.

With his other hand, Thor raises his mallet. "Ogre, while you have failed, as anticipated, to achieve a war-rior's physical strength, your ability to rescue the dragon with your creative wit, courage, and flair with the pen is a strength not to be denied. I am proud to count such an ugly ogre among my companions." He sighs. "Although never among my soldiers. Truly pathetic, indeed."

With that, Thor walks to the pouch's edge, followed by a line of headless army men, just like I drew. He kneels and looks to Lenora.

"My lady. It has been an honor serving you. The memory of the spark in your eye and the flame of your hair will warm my dark nights." Thor stands and circles his hammer one last time. "Fare thee well. May your heart find happiness. And may you always be wary of sweet-talking ogres in ugly dresses."

In a flash as quick as lightning, Thor and the men disappear into the pouch. In the same blink, my room is clean. Bed made, books put away, clothes hung, untattered. Even the char marks are gone.

"Wow," I say.

"That is some powerful magic." Lenora climbs off the bed, looking in awe at my sparkly clean room. "We'd better finish that code you started, fast. And maybe try not to break it immediately this time."

I exhale a laugh.

"Guess I'd better call Dad to come get me." She pulls her phone from her back pocket. "I'm gonna miss those little guys."

I look at my half-open closet door. All I wanted was to

get rid of that toothy lizard and flirtatious, full-of-himself superhero. But now they're gone, and I realize I might miss them too.

"Hey, Lenora," I say before she walks out the door.

"Yeah?"

"I couldn't have done this without you. Thanks."

Lenora punches my arm lightly. "Yeah, you could have." With that, she heads out the door.

She's right, I realize. I had what it took to fix my messy, magical trouble all along.

It was just more fun with her.

SUNDAY MORNING

Thump. Thump. Thump.

"Whah?" I lift my head off my pillow.

Thump. Thump. Thump.

I sit upright, my heart racing. Are Thor and Tiny T back?

"West, you awake?"

I exhale. It's just Mom knocking on my door.

"Did you finish cleaning?" She peeks her head in my bedroom. "Wait . . . what? Your room!" She comes in and walks around, running her hand along my desk. Her eyes are as large as pinwheels. "How'd you get it so clean?"

I rub the sleep out of my groggy face. "Lenora helped."

"But—the burn marks?" She kneels, running a hand across my baseball-shaped carpet.

I yawn. Vacation Brain has to think fast through my fog. "It was . . . marker. We got it out."

"Hmm . . . I've got to say, I wasn't so sure you'd get it done." Mom sits on the edge of my bed. "But now that I know what a good room-cleaner you are, I guess I can expect it always to be this clean."

Gulp. May have to do a little conjuring to keep this up.

"You have a visitor," Mom says.

"I do?"

There's a knock on my bedroom door, and Josh pokes his head in.

I bolt upright in bed. "Josh?"

"Hey, man."

Mom walks back to my door. "Have you had breakfast, Josh?"

"Oh, thanks, Mrs. Hopper. I'm good." Josh stands awkwardly, scratching at the back of his neck.

Mom leaves and shuts the door behind her.

"You're okay?" I ask.

Josh cocks his head funny at me. "Course. I mean, I have this awful itchy rash all over, but—why wouldn't I be?"

I toss off my covers and swing my legs over the edge of the bed. "Snake said you were missing."

Josh stands in the middle of my room, one hand stuffed in his shorts, the other itching his belly, swaying from side to side. "Oh."

"If you came to see the T. rex, you're too late," I say.

"You really had one? And Snake took him?"

I cross my arms. "Yup."

"I was supposed to help them." He kicks at my carpet with his left foot. "But . . . I felt bad. I didn't want to."

"Oh?"

He looks at my walls, the floor—anywhere but at me—and itches his thigh. "Yeah. Breaking into your house, taking stuff. It was . . . kind of extreme."

"Did you tell them that?"

Josh rubs his nose, looking ashamed. "I took off when they released us from school. Went the long way, through the woods, so the guys couldn't find me. I think that's where I got poison oak or something. And I just didn't answer my phone."

I think for a minute about what he's saying. And how Lenora would respond.

"So, you didn't try to stop them," I say.

"I mean, it's not like . . . How could I?"

I can think of lots of ways. Guess Josh isn't as creative a thinker as me.

"So why are you here?" I ask.

"To say . . . sorry. I mean, you kept trying to tell me about this awesome thing you found, and I blew you off."

"Because of the guys," I add.

Josh looks at his feet. "I mean, it's not like it was a believable story."

"Maybe." I shrug. "But you didn't even give me a chance."

We sit there, silently and awkwardly, for a gazillion minutes.

"So what happened yesterday?" he asks.

"Which part? When I blew up the gym or when Snake stole my T. rex?"

Josh smirks. "Sounds funny when you say it like that."

"Yeah, super funny."

"Did you blow up the gym? For real?"

I exhale. "I don't know. It's complicated."

"What happened with Snake? His dad found him, Alex, and Frankie tied up in the rec room last night. But Snake won't talk about it. Was that you?"

I think about the tiny-Viking attack. I'm sure Josh would think it was cool. But I'm not sure I care anymore. "You wouldn't believe me if I told you."

"Oh. Okay," he replies.

I pull at my pajama bottoms, then glance up, ready to ask what I've always wondered.

"Why don't you ever stick up for me?"

"Huh?" Josh asks.

"You never say, 'Hey, Snake, invite him to your party. Be nice to him.' Like that."

Josh takes in a breath. "It's not that easy. . . ."

"I thought we were friends."

"We were . . . we *are*. I just . . ." He can't even look me in the eye.

Even yesterday, I would've been relieved to hear him say we're still friends. But I've learned a lot in a few days. "Pretty sure friends stick up for each other." I stand and point at my closet. "I'm gonna get dressed now, so . . ."

"Oh. Okay. So . . . should I go? Or . . . I mean. We could do something?"

"Do something?" I ask.

"I dunno. Like, make something with the magic pouch?"

I squint. We *could* make something. I could draw that three-headed tree frog for him to show off at school, and he'd probably be my best friend forever.

But that's not how I want to make friends.

"Here's the thing," I start. "If someone was being mean to you, like Snake was to me, I'd probably not want to be friends with them. But maybe you just like Snake better than you like me. Maybe Snake is more fun. Although that's hard to imagine, since, you know—magic pouch."

"I'm sorry." Josh looks away, scratching the back of his leg. "I didn't know what to do. You act kinda different sometimes. I was afraid if I stuck up for you, they wouldn't want to be friends with me either."

"If one mistake loses a friend, maybe a true friend he never was indeed," I say, channeling Thor.

Josh just crinkles his forehead.

I continue. "Basically, you're saying you'd rather be friends with the cool, mean guys than me, just because I do weird stuff sometimes." I shrug. "So, if that's your choice . . ."

"No . . . that's not . . . choosing." He looks up. "Do *you* still want to be friends?"

I curl my bottom lip, thinking. I miss Josh. Of course I still want to be his friend. But the Josh I've seen this past year has been different. And how could I be sure he wants to be friends with me . . . or with the kid who has magic?

I draw in a deep breath, this time channeling my best Ms. Molly. "Maybe if you start acting like a *real* friend. That means *sharing* time, *understanding* what might hurt my feelings, and *sacrificing* by sticking up for each other. Then we'll see."

Josh tilts his head. "Uh. Okay?"

Just then Mom knocks on the door and pops her head in. "Hey, uh, I just got a call from the fire marshal."

Uh-oh.

Mom doesn't look mad, but sometimes she has a tricky face first, before she springs the real one on me. Especially in front of company.

"Looks like they were able to determine the cause of the explosion. Very quickly, in fact. And they were quite surprised."

Oh, I bet.

We've determined the cause of the fire was an animated fire monster, brought to life by one Westin Scott Hopper's irresponsible use of his enchanted artifact.

Here we go. The end of my life. For a second, I thought it might turn out to be a good day.

"Seems there was a slow gas leak in the gym that had started to get bigger. They're guessing something sparked the explosion—maybe even just West closing the gym door. The fire marshal said it was a very lucky thing it happened Friday when no one was in the gym, because the science fair was scheduled for yesterday. Apparently one student was planning a flaming volcano exhibit. The gym would have blown up with hundreds of people in it."

"Alex's flaming volcano!" Josh exclaims. "Whoa. He could've died. I can't wait to tell him."

Holy cow! My fire monster saved hundreds of people by blowing the gym up a day early.

"Guess it wasn't you after all." Josh stands there. Waiting for something. Maybe hoping I'll change my mind and ask him to stay.

I won't—not just yet, anyway.

"Are you sure you can't stay for breakfast?" Mom asks him.

Josh looks at me.

"No, he's gotta get going," I say.

Mom shrugs. "Get dressed and come eat then, West. Your dad will be here soon. See you next time, Josh."

"Uh, okay." Josh does a quick itch and an awkward shrug. "Bye?"

"See you at school."

He heads out, and it's a little sad, but also kind of a relief, to watch him leave.

* * *

After I get dressed in my black shorts and Red Sox shirt—Mom was able to get the grape stain out, total hero—I flop down at the kitchen table. Mom pours me a glass of orange juice and scoops some eggs onto my plate, and I gulp them down. It's been a while since I didn't have to share my breakfast.

I scarf the last bit of eggs, and my cell phone buzzes. It's Lenora. I take the phone into my bedroom.

"Hey!" Her voice is squeaky with excitement. "Did you hear? Dad said the school sent out an announcement. Everyone at the science fair would have died! You and that magic pouch are, like, superheroes."

"I wouldn't go that far," I say. "Anyway, are you going to be home later?"

"Yup. Just shoveling manure all day. Would love the help."

"Gross. I'll be over after Dad picks me up."

"See ya."

I grab my sketchpad and start drawing while I wait. The wooden box with the pouch and Marty's drawings sit beside me at my desk. Even though using the magic without clearing it with Lenora is breaking the one and only rule in my code, I'm going to cheat this once—for good reason.

When I finish, I tear the sketch off the pad and lift the lid of the box to put it inside. I had to do it mostly from memory, but I think I got it. I pull out Marty's drawings to tuck inside my desk drawer for safekeeping, and as I do, the one on top catches my eye. I didn't really look at it before—too distracted with the plane ticket and Mustang—but it's a scene from Uncle Marty's living room. I recognize the ugly crocodile painting over the sofa. There's also a guy, who looks a lot like Uncle Marty, putting a red sock on his foot.

I study the drawing closely and realize . . . it's not a red sock.

"Holy magic pouch!" I exclaim.

I sit there for a minute with my mouth ajar, then remember to breathe. If this drawing is what I think it is, then Uncle Marty sent *himself* to the Other Realm. And if he really went into the pouch, then Uncle Marty's *own* Vacation Brain is on another planet.

But also . . . it means he could still be alive. And that is an excellent possibility. I wonder if he'll run into Thor. That would be seriously awesome. More importantly, I wonder if he wants to come back. If he even *can* come back.

Mom knocks, and I put Marty's drawings back and close the box. "Come in."

She enters and leans over my shoulder. "Dad's on his way. You have your stuff ready?" She points to my drawing. "Hey, that's adorable. You're such a good artist."

I smile back at her. "Thanks."

"We could put that one in the charter-school application."

"Nope." I turn around. "I'm not going. Not to that

school or Dad's private one. I want to do Mr. Lowde's art club, and I want to stay with Lenora."

Mom crosses her arms, her jaw slack. "But the mortgage. Your dad—"

I put up a hand. "I'd rather not hear about that stuff, Mom. It's between you and Dad." Dad's horn beeps outside. "Talk to him. I don't want to move. Gotta go. See you next Sunday."

I scoop up the sketch and box, grab my stuff, and kiss Mom's cheek. There's no way I'm giving up this sketch for some application. It's for Lenora.

SUNDAY AFTERNOON

Dad and I pull up to Lenora's house, and Ned waves to us from the barn.

"You can stop here, Dad. You sure it's okay if I hang with her for a bit?"

Dad brings the Evidence to a stop and leaves the engine running. "Text me when you're done. I'll come get you."

"We going to Gram's later?"

"Sure thing, kiddo." He puts his hand on the side of my baseball cap, and I can feel his thick, warm fingers over my ear. I think he feels bad about getting mad at me for the gym when it wasn't my fault—technically.

"Dad. Um. About school?"

"What about it?"

"I know we just had a pile of trouble with the explosion and all, but . . . I really want to stay at my school." I tense, waiting for his reply.

"Buddy. I know the fire wasn't you, but still. You need more discipline. You need to know the consequences of your impulsive actions," he says firmly.

"Dad, I don't mean to be trouble. I promise. When you get mad, it just makes me feel worse about doing something I couldn't control. I'd do it the right way the first time, if I could. Really. And if I stay at my school, there's an art club I can join. I'm really good at art. I want to feel proud of what I do for a change."

Dad bites on his lower lip, studying me.

"Would you at least talk to Mom about it, please? And not in a fighting way?"

"Uh . . ."

"Please? Can we just talk about it? But not now. Lenora's waiting."

Dad nods. "I'll think about it."

I'm not exactly sure what will happen, but at least it isn't a *no*. "Okay." I open the car door. "Love you, Dad. See you later."

"Love you too."

I slam the door and run toward the barn with my

sketch. The magic pouch and wooden box are both tucked safely in my backpack. I have to wait until Mr. Pickering goes over by the horse corral, so he can't see what I'm up to. When I'm done, I smile. Lenora is going to love it. I hope.

I run up to the house and knock on the old door. This time, Lenora answers herself.

"What took you so long? You missed all the manure." She tugs on my arm. "Come in."

I pull her in the opposite direction. "No, you come with me."

We start walking down the long, gravel driveway.

"What are you up to?" she asks.

"You'll see."

Lenora notices what I'm carrying. "You brought the wooden box? And the pouch?"

We stop, and I thrust the wooden box toward her. "Here. Take it."

"Huh?"

"To be perfectly safe, the new first order of the code should be that you keep this instead of me." I push the box at her until she grabs hold of it. "The second order can be that I have to clear its use with you."

"Why?"

"Because. It doesn't work for you. That way there's no

temptation. With Vacation Brain, I'll be drawing stuff in the middle of the night. It'll start with me acing tests, then money, a brand-new Red Sox jersey. But before long, who knows? Cranky Steve will show up with purple hair and no nose one day. Don't get me started about what I could do to Mr. Widelot. It's Vacation Brain we're talking about."

Lenora nods. "That's very mature of you, West."

I lift a shoulder. "It's the only time Brain stuck around to make a good decision, I guess. Come look, though. You'll see exactly why I shouldn't keep this magic in my room."

We keep walking, but Lenora gets strangely quiet—especially for Lenora. The crunch of our feet on tiny rocks is the only sound.

"Are you okay?" I ask.

"Yeah." She pauses. "I told my dad I wanted to talk about my mom."

"Oh. What'd he say?"

"We haven't talked yet. He got all teary, but he agreed. Said we could go for a walk through the fields later, just us, and talk about her." She has a wide smile, like it's her birthday and the first day of summer.

"That's good."

She falls quiet again.

"West?" she says, almost choking as she speaks.

"Yeah?"

"I wanted to say . . . thanks. Seeing you tackle your troubles head-on gave me the courage to ask my dad for what I need."

I drop my glance to the gravelly path and keep walking. If I stop, she might try to hug me. Then I turn, walking backward at a quick pace. "Don't thank me yet! Come on!"

I bolt to the chicken coop, and she follows.

"What are you up to?" Lenora pretends to be worried, but she's all smiles.

I stop in front of the gate. The chicken coop is a small, wired pen with a bunch of spotted brown and red chickens waddling around. Toward the back, there's a little shed where the chickens sleep at night with a ramp right up the middle.

Lenora puts her hands on her hips. "My chicken coop. So what?"

"So look inside the shed."

She gives me a curious look but pushes at the wire gate and shoos the chickens away. I follow as Lenora walks to the shed and opens the small wood door. Inside, resting on straw, is a six-inch white chicken. Not a baby chick. A full-grown mini chicken.

Lenora drops the wooden box at her feet and gasps. "Is that—"

"Bobbie. Kind of."

Lenora draws in an excited breath and pulls the small chicken out, cuddling it in her palm. "It's mini Bobbie! How—"

"I saw the picture of her in your bedroom. I drew her the best I could. I know I broke our code, and I know it's not *exactly* Bobbie, but—"

"It's really close." She lifts him up to inspect. "Even prettier." There's a tear in her eye.

"He'll probably grow, like Tiny T did. Just in time for the County Fair. Just . . . keep her away from Grannie."

Lenora laughs and nuzzles her nose into the feathers on mini Bobbie's back.

I look at the ground and kick at the dirt. "I couldn't give you your mom, so . . ."

"So you made me a zombie chicken." She starts to cry, real tears streaming tracks through the dust on her face.

I tense. "You don't like it?"

Lenora shakes her head, then throws an arm around me, careful not to squish mini Bobbie, and buries her head in my neck. It gets wet from her tears.

"I love her. And you're right. I should keep this." She taps her foot on the box. "And *I* was right. You are so *not* boring." She pulls back as mini Bobbie squirms in her palm, and she giggles. "But, man, oh, man, *are* you trouble!"

I exhale, relieved I didn't mess up. Because yeah—sometimes Brain is off at a luau when I need him, and yeah, sometimes I do stuff I don't mean to. But that's not all I am. I'm all sorts of other cool things too: curious, adventurous, creative . . . and a good friend.

So I'm trouble all right.

But maybe just trouble with a tiny t.

ACKNOWLEDGEMENTS

When I was ten years old, I wrote a fan letter to an author, Carolyn Sheehan, and she wrote back, becoming my lifelong pen pal. She's passed from this world now, but for me, her letters were the stuff of magic from the Other Realm. She inspired my dream of being a writer and changed my life. (In fact, it was on a plane trip to visit her that I met my husband!)

Since then, a lot of friends have helped me figure out the magic of writing this book. My kids' amazing teacher, Jessica Whitehouse, and her son, Felix; Miles and Aiden Squiers, Milo Gillies, Jesse Mosher, and especially Ismael Kusumaatmadja; the best math teacher, Mr. Widelock, for the fun misuse of his name; my incredible, giving, and detailed critique partners, Dean Gloster and Sally Pla— thank you all.

For their enduring and unwavering friendship, critiques, and all things writing, I love my YAMS and Story Sisters, especially Shells Legoullon, Lisa Schulman, Nikki Garcia, and Jennifer Alvarez. Also Darcy Rosenblatt, Amanda Conran, Jennifer Gennari, and the gang at the Society of Children's Book Writers and Illustrators (SCBWI).

Thank you to The Book Passage, my local indie store, for existing and for your incredible support for writers. It was in Andrea Alban's writer's workshop that I wrote the first chapter.

For my English teachers, Bruce Schauble and George Farrell, your early faith in me was instrumental. Thank you Randi Barshack—now go finish your book!

To my muse, best friend, and partner-in-crime, Linda Stutz—girlfriend, thank you and I love you. For the late Bill Turnage, who made me a better writer and was my greatest champion—man, I miss you.

I could not have conjured up a better literary agent than the amazing Caryn Wiseman at the Andrea Brown Literary Agency. Thank you for loving and championing Westin as much as I do and for making me take out the Norwegian elves—you are an ever-shining star, as is your assistant, Alison Nolan. To the team at Capstone: Michelle Bisson, Hilary Wacholz, and especially my patient and keen-eyed editor, Alison Deering. I am grateful for your vision and efforts on behalf of this book.

Although we've never met, a special thanks to my heroes, Russell Barkley, David Nowell, and Stephen Hinshaw, whose research and writings on ADHD helped inform me as a clinician. And you too, Holly Seerley.

Thanks to the folks at ADDitude for letting me blog. ADHD is a very real, very painful, and quite-misunderstood diagnosis. It is my sincere hope that through Westin's lighthearted adventures, readers will recognize themselves and feel seen—or recognize another and finally understand.

To my family—the squirrely, loud, loving, and funny lot of you. Mom, you're my wings. J, you're basically the hot air underneath. Jim, you too. Dad, I miss you and wish you could see your little girl in print.

To my kids, you are my magic. Sabrina—your amazing crayon mermaid on the wall and adventures in sheet-cutting were the seeds of Westin's story. You're my favorite.

Maclean—aka, Superfast Punching Man—no, this book is not about you, and you're also my favorite. Tabitha—you were Westin's first real friend. Thank you for letting me read this to you chapter by chapter and telling me where it was boring. You are my favorite.

And finally, to my loving and patient husband, who indulges my passion for writing, cheerleads me endlessly, and is always ready to rub my weary shoulders—I love you like the wind.

BOBBIE THE CHICKEN, BY SABRINA SAUNDERS

ABOUT THE AUTHOR

Merriam Sarcia Saunders, LMFT, is a family therapist and author of the picture books *My Whirling, Twirling Motor* and *My Wandering, Dreaming Mind*, both affirming stories about children with ADHD. Merriam and her husband live in Northern California with their three kids, one silly lab, and a tiny chihuahua with no teeth. This is her first novel. To learn more about Merriam, visit merriamsbooks.com.